William Clark Russell

The Tale of the Ten

Vol. 1

William Clark Russell

The Tale of the Ten
Vol. 1

ISBN/EAN: 9783337347055

Printed in Europe, USA, Canada, Australia, Japan

Cover: Foto ©Andreas Hilbeck / pixelio.de

More available books at **www.hansebooks.com**

THE TALE OF THE TEN

A SALT-WATER ROMANCE

BY

W. CLARK RUSSELL

AUTHOR OF
'THE WRECK OF THE GROSVENOR' 'MY SHIPMATE LOUISE'
'THE CONVICT SHIP' ETC.

IN THREE VOLUMES—VOL. I.

LONDON
CHATTO & WINDUS, PICCADILLY
1896

PRINTED BY
SPOTTISWOODE AND CO., NEW-STREET SQUARE
LONDON

CONTENTS

OF

THE FIRST VOLUME

THE TALE OF THE TEN

CHAPTER I

THE BARQUE 'QUEEN'

ONE moonlight night two men stood at the
extremity of a point of land that jutted into
the black ripple of Sydney Bay. The moon
rode high and rained a light that floated in
the air in a mist of splendour; the vision
was overwhelmed by the brilliance; the dark
shore on either hand the spot where the two
men stood sank into visionary streaks a little
distance from them, and looking across
Sydney Bay was like being at sea.

The Circular Quay had not been built in
those days: ships lay moored in creeks; and

here and there you caught a glimpse as of a thundercloud of mast and spar interlaced and knitted into deep shadow, here and there touched into silver gleams. In the Bay the riding lights of ships winked against the flooding moonlight weak as fireflies.

A ship rode opposite the men; she was perhaps three-quarters of a mile distant, easily to be distinguished as a handsome little barque, with all her sea-gear rove and her sails stowed, as though just arrived or shortly departing. The men looked at her whilst they quietly conversed. Past her this moment there went floating, dim as a column of vapour, a large ship newly arrived from the old country. In a few minutes she broke up the silence in the Bay by the roar of iron links swept through iron, and by the halloing and bawling of men as the sails melted in the moonlight into wreaths and festoons delicate as vapour.

It was ten o'clock. Some chimes came in

faint strains from Sydney town. They were caught up by the ships' bells, and a pretty noise of tinkling, with clearer, deeper, nearer notes from some throats of metal up the creek past the men, trembled in a fairy music across the waters. Here and there upon the breast of the Bay crept some little shadow of boat, framed in a dim glitter of phosphor that would have been a bright light had the moon been dark. Scarcely had the last of the ships' bells rung out ten o'clock when a noise of oars caught the attention of the men.

' Here he comes,' said one of them, straining his eyes in the direction of the sound under the sharp of his hand as though the sun was in the sky.

' No, no,' answered the other gruffly; ' why, Trollope, that noise means a gunwale full of tholes. You'll not see Hankey till he's here.'

As the man spoke these words, both of them articulating in accents of refinement, a low, long white boat came close in out of the haze of the moonlight with a man in the stern-sheets, who stood up on catching sight of the figures upon the strip of land, apparently staring at them. You saw a gleam of buttons on his frock-coat, and the six men who were bowing leisurely on the thwarts were uniformly apparelled.

'Oars!' cried the man in the stern-sheets.

The boat floated to a stand right abreast the creek, into whose yawning mouth, gloom ing swiftly out of the silver into dusk, thickened by the masts and rigging of ships, the man continued to stare for some moments as though in expectation. The two men down on the point where the water came strumming with a guitar-like note in black ripples, watched him.

'What is that boat?' said one of them.

'Either the harbour guard-boat, or she belongs to a man-of-war,' answered the other.

'What have they got the scent of? On

the track of deserters, perhaps. Or keeping a bright look-out on what's yonder, eh?' and the speaker nodded in the direction of the barque.

The man in the stern-sheets resumed his seat, the oars were leisurely dipped, and the boat vanished in the vaporous sheen.

Five minutes after she was out of sight, a black spot showed close in on a line with the barque. It enlarged swiftly into a little boat, with a man sculling her. He was alone. He drove the boat a short way up the creek, where the brine brimmed without break of ripple, and jumped out, keeping a hold of his boat by her painter. The others joined him.

'Well, Hankey, what's the news?'

'I've been an hour with Poole, and have corkscrewed out of him as much as I think is to be got. A couple of bottles of champagne made him chatty, and the captain was ashore, and the chief mate indisposed in his cabin.

There are a few passengers on board. She
sails to-morrow at two, and seemed to me,
whilst she lies in the moonlight, as I walked
her deck, the prettiest little craft that was
ever handled by a sailor. Easily to be worked
in my judgment by half-a-dozen men. Her
yards are square for her size, but I'd under-
take to roll up her maintopsail, blowing hard,
with three men.'

The others listened eagerly. The man
spoke with an educated accent. The three of
them suggested the broken officer, the gentleman who had come to the colonies for the
gold rush, who had failed, and made shift for
his life in twenty different directions, sailoris-
ing seemingly being one of them, as might be
inferred at all events from Mr. Hankey's talk
of topsails, and the other's appreciative understanding of his words.

'Has she an arms-chest?' said one of
them.

'Yes.'

' Where stowed?'

'In the second mate's cabin. Rather mean,' continued the speaker, ' as an arms' chest : contents, a few cutlasses, refuse Navy goods, a few old pistols, and maybe a sheaf of short blunderbusses. The Scotch owners don't put money into their arms-chest,' he added with a sudden laugh.

' But this is your surmise?' said one of them; 'otherwise the chest may be handsomely stocked.'

The gentleman gave the painter of the boat to one of his friends to hold whilst he pulled out a short pipe.

'Let them be of to-day's pattern and purchase,' said the man who had received the boat's painter, ' the mate's porthole is big enough to pass them through, I suppose?'

'Any ammunition?' said the third man, speaking with a delicate accent and a slight lisp.

'Well, now I forgot to ask that question,' was the answer.

'How many go to the crew?' said one of them.

'Of foremast hands, eleven. They can't muster more. The full complement is eighteen. As fast as the chaps sign they pocket a month's advance and desert, and the police can do nothing for the captain. The second mate told me that the *Queen* hauled out today merely for the better chance of keeping the men aboard. They have given special instructions to the guard boat to keep a watch through the night.'

'She has just passed,' said one.

'A six-oared arrangement in charge of a Cornstalker in buttons. She saw my boat hanging on the barque's quarter, and hailed; the second mate looked over and said it was all right, I was his friend, and was not to be troubled should they fall in with me sculling ashore.'

'There's no mistake, I hope,' said the gentleman, who slightly lisped, ' as to its being safely on board?'

'Poole, when the champagne mounted, bragged of it,' was the reply. ' "Only think," said the man, laying his hand upon my arm with a silly grin, " even Anson's Jack Spaniards went ragged in comparison with us!" " Bosh!" said I. " It's a horrible big trust though," said he. " If some of our pier-head jumpers get the breeze of it, we may need to polish our irons." I asked him in a dawdling, sleepy way, looking at the moonlight on the water, as if I could think of nothing but the poetry of this romantic scene'—the gentleman with the lisp here interrupted with a laugh—'where they stowed the thing for the best safe-keeping of it. " Oh, confound it," he answered, " I ought to know, for I had the handling of it. It's in a strong room, specially built, just abaft the mainmast, in the main-hold. The wool's snugged all around it;

a stupid blunder in the packing," said he, whilst I filled his glass, " for suppose spontaneous combustion, the wool glowing under battened hatches, and the ship living for days, as ships *do* live in such a state, and then making port ; why," cried he, emptying his glass, " it would be all liquor, and we'd be pumping it out along with the water." '

'She is a lovely sight in this light,' said the man named Trollope, his voice softening as his eyes went to the little barque. 'It was in such another as she that I came out at a shilling a month. *She* could pile it to the cathead to a song of thirteen knots in a topgallant breeze. Yet there's something yonder,' said he with a nod of his head across the Bay, 'that could give her a towrope and not know it.'

The three men stood viewing the scene for some minutes in silence. The moonlight was upon them, and their shadows were defined with such amazing sharpness that they might have been six men, three sleeping at the others' feet. Trollope began to whistle, then rounded on his heel.

'How is London looking at this moment, I wonder?' said he. 'If all comes off right, it's my home. There's no other place in the world to live in, and I know the world.'

'I'm off,' said the man who had come from the barque; 'shall I scull you to the steps?'

They got into the little boat, two sitting low in her, and she glided quietly up the creek where some ships were lying. As she vanished the barque's bell struck five—half-past ten. The notes sounded like a flute, and in a minute or two the stillness was broken by a clanging that, to a fancy listening behind closed eyes, might have made a Sabbath morn in England of that Australian night of moon and stars.

*   *   *   *

The barque *Queen* had been advertised

to sail from Sydney three weeks before she finally started.   Her detention had been owing to the captain's difficulty in getting men, or keeping those who signed the articles.   She was insufficiently manned, as it was, for a barque of her tonnage in those days, of single topsails and liberal labour.

The captain grew mad with impatience. Some of the passengers seemed to be looking about for other ships sailing for Europe. Fortunately for the *Queen* all other vessels were in the same quandary.   At last the mate of this composite barque got together a wild, rugged, ragged, and hairy crew—objects that had been starved out of the gold fields, wretches who for nights had slept like dead soldiers on the field of glory.   Then lest even *they* should tumble ashore and vanish whilst the captain was eating his lunch and the mate was overhauling the live stock with the butcher, the ship was hurriedly warped out: shore-fasts were let go, capstans manned, and in a few minutes the beautiful little fabric was sliding needle-like before a pleasant breeze under a wing or two of white cloth for the anchorage where she was now lying.

At two o'clock in the afternoon of the day following that on which she left her berth, the *Queen* got under way. Her destination was London. It was calculated she would cover the distance in seventy-five days. She had made the run out in eighty, which was faster than steam, as steam *then* was.

The windlass was manned, and a chorus with some fire and spirit in it rang over the bush that darkened the nearer shore where a white villa or two gleamed. There blew a fine fair sailing breeze, rich with Australian sunshine and the blue of the heavens, and fragrant as a nosegay. The slop chest had been overhauled in the morning; the crew had washed themselves and put on clean shirts, and now showed as a fairly respectable body of English seamen. They had slept in bunks, they had eaten heartily of the ship's food. The work they had been put to had taken the kinks out of their backs and the turns out of their arms and legs, and they felt something like men as they thought of London river and hove in the iron links one by one to the cheery yells of the mate looking over the bows, and to their own roaring heartening chorus of 'Time for us to go.'

Two or three boats were making shore-wards from the ship, and men and women standing up in them waved responsive signals of farewell to the motions of some of the passengers on the poop. The number of people bound homewards in the *Queen* numbered in all, ladies and gentlemen, nineteen. All were on deck as the anchor was lifted from the ground, and the barque, to the impulse of her jib and foretopsail, rounded slowly to her course. They looked a shipload, and seemed nearly all men. Indeed, there were but seven ladies, one the wife of a colonial merchant,

Mrs. James Dent, others a Mrs. Holroyd and her daughter Edith, Miss Margaret Mansel, a fine young woman with dark eyes and a pensive musing air. The pilot had charge of the ship, and the captain walked the deck apart, everybody easily seeing that he was full of the business of the vessel and wished to be alone.

He was a type of the skipper that has vanished off the face of the waters. His face was the colour of the freshly sawn end of a balk of mahogany, which uncommon hue was accentuated by his snow-white hair and whiskers. His grey eyes were set deep in his head; long years of staring into hard weather had berthed them below their natural moorings, and you wondered how he saw out of two such holes. His legs had been arched by years of the heaving plank. He wore the tall hat of the London streets, and this was his headgear whether in the roaring gale of the Horn or the roasting calm of the Doldrums.

The ship's head was now fair for the open, and they were making sail upon her as fast as they could set it. There is no prettier sight than that of such a barque as this getting under way and slowly whitening the blue with the light of her canvas. The topsails fall, the yards are hoisted, topgallant sails swell as their clews slide to the yardarms, the fore-course arches its foot of snow, beyond are the jibs tremorless as the wings of the poised albatross, arching to the fishing-rod end of the flying jibboom; the whole fabric is clothed. She floats in beauty, gay with the lights of the day; a delicate line of pearl, lustrous as the inside of a shell, trembles from her cutwater along her metal sheathing and goes away in a little wake whose extremity invited many an eye aboard this ship to the delicious sweetness of the island-studded bay they were leaving.

Some of the passengers were well worth observing. They play a large part in this traditionary and remarkable story of the sea, and a few of them may be introduced at once whilst the barque is making for the Heads. A man is leaning over the low brass rail that protects the poop from the fall of the quarter-deck; he pulls a heavy black moustache whilst he seems to be gazing ahead; he would be an extremely handsome man if it were not that he has a most pronounced turn-up nose. His looks are manly, his air frank, he is broadly built and stands above six foot. You would judge that he had served in the army by his posture even as he leaned. A sailor when he leans sprawls from breech to heels, and the rest is as slack as his shirt collar. On the other hand, a soldier never lounges.

A little distance from him, but not apparently acquainted with the man, stood another with a broken military cut; this person was of medium height, with strong whiskers shooting with an air of briskness into their

own dead blackness. He too was good-looking, straight-nosed, had a well-bred look, a
dark eye, quiet and searching. His clothes
were indeed too new. They lacked that come-
liness of wear which George Eliot commends.
But who would notice such a thing in a man
going home from Australia?

A third gentleman leans against the port-
rail; his little blue eyes, weak with the damp
of drink, are fixed upon Miss Margaret Mansel,
who is talking to Mrs. Holroyd and her
daughter on the other side of the deck. He
is a biggish man of the fat and rolling sort,
yellow-haired, with a faint buttercup fluff of
moustache which one hand or the other is for
ever haunting. These three men were last
night standing upon a slip of land in Sydney
Harbour and admiring the barque by the
light of the moon and the scene of the bay
under the stars. Who could have guessed by
their conversation then that they had booked
as passengers by the *Queen*?

The tall man with the heavy black moustache was Captain Henry Trollope ; the second Mr. Paul Hankey, and the fat fellow at the rail, Alexander Burn.

Another passenger at whom the ladies occasionally glanced askance was Mr. Sampson Masters : at a little distance his was as perfect a face as you could figure. When he drew close his features showed blistered and pocked by drink and dissipation. He stood near the wheel, looking from under the brim of a white felt hat with a black hatband, right up at the canvas, yet with glances any sailor would have seen were critical.

There were other men, several ; one was a little chap, Mr. William Storr, an auctioneer going home after doing business in the Antipodes. His round, lightly whiskered face was enthusiastic with the sense of departure and the beauty of the scene. Close beside him stood a large man who had booked his passage by the name of Mark Davenire : he wore a heavy silver chain upon his bright green waistcoat, and his cabbage-tree hat was tilted upon his nose, whilst his eyes somewhat stealthily travelled round about.

The shyness peculiar to Englishmen was noticeable amongst the passengers at the start. The ladies, it is true, fluttered before long into conversation with one another, but the men held off; which was strange in three of them at all events, for they had seemed on very good terms on the previous night.

'Good gracious me!' suddenly exclaimed Mrs. James Dent, whose black hair was plastered down her cheeks and over the back of her ears in the early Victorian style, 'isn't that an open boat out there?'

She pointed with a hand that sparkled. The ship was now close in with the entrance to Sydney Bay, and the object the lady pointed at sank and rolled, and wallowed about three-quarters of a mile distant right ahead. Everybody drew to the side to look.

Captain Trollope fixed a glass in his eye.
Captain Benson, the white-haired skipper,
took the ship's telescope from its brackets
and gazed with attention.

'I hope you will pass her close,' said Mrs.
Dent.

'She shall slide alongside of us, madam,'
answered the captain.

'What's there in an open boat,' said Mrs.
Storr taking her husband's arm and towering
by help of an oddly shaped hat to nearly half
a head above her husband, 'to make the
ocean seem more desolate than when there's
nothing in sight?'

'Ha!' exclaimed Mr. Burn waddling up
to the little group that had gathered about
the captain, and expanding his 'ha!' in a fat
beery sigh, 'there's a depth of meaning in
that question, and it shows the ocean in a new
light.'

Mr. Storr looked at him suspiciously; the
lady smiled and said, 'When we came out in

the *Light of the Age* we fell in with an abandoned ship. She made the ocean look a horrible desert. The same effect is produced by that small boat there.'

' You will find the reason to be this,' said Mr. Burn with a gentlemanly though an oozy accent; ' great fields of solitude need accentuation to the eye. A single object achieves this. A single star makes the heavens look as wide again. A lonely wreck furnishes the imagination with a starting point for measuring the prodigious distances of the ocean.'

He spoke as though he had been an actor in his day.

Captain Trollope glanced at Mr. Burn through his glass, and then turned his head with a smile which his moustache effectually hid. Others, such as Mr. Davenire, Mr. Caldwell, a dark-faced, black-bearded, Jewish-looking man, and one or two others also listened with an air of faint amusement.

'But there's such a plenty of land about,' continued Mrs. Storr, who was evidently gratified by the attention she appeared to be receiving from most of the gentlemen, ' and still that open boat makes the sea look more lonely than a moor by moonlight, with the arm of a gibbet dangling a dead man over the snow.'

This vigorous image seemed greatly to impress Mr. Burn, whose hands plied his little moustache with a sudden vehemence.

' There's an open boat right under the bow, sir,' shouted the mate from the forecastle.

As the boat slided by a strange murmur from the ship accompanied her. She was a whaleboat, had probably belonged to a foreign whaler, and in the bottom of her lay two dead men, one with his teeth in the throat of the other, as though, wanting a knife, or too feeble to use one, he had sought in his agony to quench his thirst thus.

But it was a sight common enough at sea. There are few who have used the ocean who cannot speak of it as something they have seen or suffered. How should any man but a sailor understand such things? Most of the ladies hid their faces and recoiled from the rail: some of the gentlemen turned pale, and Mr. Burn looked sick. But it was for the rude hearts forward to give the true signification of the thing that had now circled into the wake, tumbling in its ghastly loneliness upon the waters broken by the ship's passage. Oh, what did it not speak? The long nights, the burning days it told of, the empty breaker, the glazing eye, the phantasm of a cold valley, so sweet with the musical babble of running rivulets, that the froth at the lip of the deluded wretch flaked afresh!

There was nothing to be read in the old skipper's face as he put the glass down. Mr. Dent looking at the white-haired seaman with something of a determined manner, as though

he summoned resolution to his utterance, exclaimed, ' I wish we hadn't fallen in with that
boat. It's an unlucky sign to stumble over a
corpse on the threshold of a journey.'

' Those bodies are well clear of the ship,
sir,' answered the captain. ' They'll not hurt
you.'

' Granted,' exclaimed one of the passengers
with small eyes and a lifting yet half-concealed
sort of grin that made his face loathsome for
self-complacency, ' but the gentleman refers
to the sentiment of the thing, not the fact of
it. I wonder that you, captain, as a sailor
are not superstitious. The trade is the most
gullible in the world.'

The captain looked at the speaker's boots
and then aloft at his ship.

' I shan't be able to eat any dinner after
that sight,' exclaimed Captain Trollope strolling up to Mr. Storr.

As though to test him, the first dinner-bell
rang, and even then more than one eye had

taken notice of a leaning shaft of brilliant
canvas hanging steadily right astern past the
boat, with a fulness of cloths and a steadfast-
ness of posture that gave one the idea of
pursuit.

CHAPTER II

THE CHASE

THE passengers dined by the light of a splendid sunset, which streamed through porthole and skylights, glittering in crimson scars in the gleaming furniture of the table, and glorifying by one wavering spoke of misty light the figure of the white-headed skipper; for the lamps were already burning, so as to take up the evening tale when the sun had gone.

It was one of those pictures of shipboard hospitality you will seldom, or never, meet upon the high seas in these days. Now, the great steamship splits its hundreds into twenty tables, and the captain is a mere detail of buttons and lace, faint and dim in distance as host, and high and lonely as master. In the days of the *Queen* the passengers of a ship formed a family party; they sat in rows; the captain at the top could answer the question put to him by the man at the bottom; when people got to know each other therefore, conversation at meal-times was easily general.

A couple of stewards moved along the line of diners; they each wore camlet jackets; each was wonderfully nimble of limb. Through the windows you heard the noise of passing waters, like the sound of a thaw at night in an open country.

When all were seated and every passenger had taken his and her place this first day— for the swell was light, the movement rhythmic, and then again all were seasoned travellers—the captain glanced down the line of faces on either hand, and for an instant seemed struck by the appearance of the people he was to navigate to England. The number of men seemed to make the ladies comparatively few, yet there were seven of that sex to break the male array into colours of garments and caps.

It was not Mr. James Dent nor yet Mr. William Storr who took the eye of the old skipper in that swift momentary glance of his to port and starboard down the table. He was impressed by a certain odd similitude as of a sort of turf or horsey family likeness; it was a kind of professional resemblance as in clean-shaven actors for example; but how to define it? Certainly Captain Trollope was as different looking a man from Mr. Burn, as Mr. Shannon with his large protruding blue eyes and ginger beard was from the black and sullen-faced Mr. Caldwell. But old Benson was no hand at defining. Military failures at home and in the Colonies, thought he as he yawned at a spoonful of soup; they had paid their fares, some forty, some fifty guineas apiece, and without exception seemed a body of very gentlemanly men.

At the foot of the table sat the chief officer, Mr. Matthews, a brown man with a red curl of beard, and a shade of paleness in his complexion as from recent illness. On his left was the ship's surgeon, and on the other hand Mr. Paul Hankey. Little was said at the start. Most of the men appeared to eye each other critically, as though they met for the first time. Mr. William Storr who, as an auctioneer, should have been able at least to feel the pulse of the company, tried to start a conversation on the subject of the boat, but was silenced by many looks of aversion from the ladies, and by the gentleman named Cavendish asking with an odd grin :

'Are you in the interest of the owners on board this ship, sir ? '

'I don't understand you,' answered Mr. Storr.

'Pooh !' said Mr. Masters, who looked uncommonly handsome in the deceptive radiance of sunset and lamplight, glancing as he spoke at Miss Margaret Mansel, 'the gentle-man means that you want to save the cabin table.'

Mr. Storr stared stupidly for a further explanation.

'Pray,' said Mr. Hankey in a very airy gentlemanly tone, addressing the mate, Mr. Matthews, 'where does Mr. Poole, the second mate, dine?'

'Here, when the others have finished and I have gone on deck,' answered the mate.

'I came out with that gentleman in the *Golden Ball*, said Mr. Hankey; 'he was third mate of her. I should say a better sailor never jockeyed a yardarm.'

'That's a good expression,' said Mr. Mat-thews, smiling slowly.

'Were you ever at sea professionally?' inquired the surgeon.

'Ask no questions of a man who has sought luck in Australia,' answered Hankey with a bland smile and a bow.

Here the black, Jewish-looking man named Caldwell broke in :

'I did not receive much encouragement when I came out. They told me that last voyage the son of a baronet, whose father lived in a mansion in Hyde Park, had sailed as saloon passenger for the gold rush; the ship arrived, and was within a day or two of her sailing for England full up with wool, when the midshipman at the gangway saw a scarecrow crawl over the side. It touched the remains of its hat, its rags fluttered, its face was of a beastly yellow, and hollow with famine and suffering. "Don't you remember me?" it sighed. The midshipman, who was without sentiment, said "No." The scarecrow named himself. He was the baronet's son. He had been knocking about for three months, had found no gold, could get no food, had pawned himself down to his socks, and had come to beg a passage home. They took pity on the poor devil, and gave him an under-steward's berth; that is, he was not even thought good enough to wait at the table at which he had formerly sat. He had to take the dirty dishes forward to the galley and wash them. Those were encouraging yarns to a man like me.'

He was about to add something, but choked the words down with a glass of wine.

The conversation prospered after this. Mr. Caldwell's anecdote set the others chatting. Those who had looked somewhat askance at one another now fell into talk, and the captain found himself at the head of a table full of people who promised on the whole to form an agreeable and sociable party. There was some reference to gold.

'Who knows the latest value of the nugget?' said Mr. Davenire, the big man with the bright waistcoat and silver chain.

'Three pound to three pun' one per ounce,' answered Mr. Dent.

'It was the story of Hargreaves' discovery

that brought me out here,' said one of the gentlemen, named Mr. Peter Johnson. 'That fellow, I mean, who up in Bathurst knocked a hundredweight of gold worth four thousand pounds out of a rock. Good angels, what joy for Hargreaves!'

'Did the gold rush bring *you* out?' said Mr. Masters, languishing across the table as he addressed Miss Mansel.

'I came to better myself as a governess, and am driven home again by colonial indifference to my few gifts,' said the girl, blushing.

'One and all, one and all!' exclaimed Captain Trollope.

'The colonies are mere rat-traps for the catching of the vermin of the old country,' said Mr. Storr.

'Many suicides happen in your experience, captain, during your runs home since the gold find?' inquired Mr. Hankey.

'One man died suddenly last voyage,'

answered the old skipper. 'We thought it was suicide till the doctor discovered that ardent spirits had burnt up his viscera. Why should a man kill himself,' he continued thoughtfully, looking at Mrs. Holroyd, 'when he has paid his passage, and will get home by waiting?'

Nobody seemed disposed to consider the point, and shortly afterwards the whole of the passengers went on deck.

It was now evening, a fine, clear dusk, full of stars, and a moon over the port-bow. The breeze had scanted, yet the sails slept, and the ripples spread out thin as silver harpstrings from the bows. The awnings had been furled, and the dew sparkled crisply on rail and binnacle-hood. The ocean swept in a measureless shadow to the stars, and more than one passenger, particularly the ladies, shuddered when the company passed through the companion-way on deck, and found the beauty of the night tragic with the tiny ark of horror that was somewhere astern.

The second mate, Poole, before diving to his dinner saluted the captain.

'Nothing in sight, sir, but a small sail right in our wake, scarcely visible even with the night glass. But I'm not sure that she didn't throw up a blue ball a few minutes ago.'

'Bring me the glass,' said the captain. The second mate then went to dinner, and the captain, putting down the glass, tucked Mrs. and Miss Holroyd under his arms and walked the weather side of the poop.

The men lolled about. Mr. Cavendish, whose expression was an objectionable small-eyed grin of self-complacency, got hold of Miss Mansel. Mr. Burn talked with great politeness to Mrs. James Dent and her daughter. Some of the fellows went down on to the quarter-deck where smoking was permitted, and hung in groups chatting plea-

santly, as though a single dinner aboard the
Queen had made them all good friends.

The close of the dog-watches in fine
weather is the pleasantest hour of the day at
sea. The moonlight ripples on the waters,
the breeze is soft, and the stars shine purely.
The shadows of those who sit or stand fan
slowly with the movements of the ship. This
was a very perfect night. The dust of the
meteor sailed across the Southern Cross, and
the slow passage of the scintillant smoke
seemed to deepen to the eye the hush in the
heavenly solitudes. Forward some man was
playing a concertina softly. Several of the
passengers, including Captain Trollope,
Davenire, Caldwell, and Hankey, went along
as far as the galley, and appeared to listen.
Here they found a couple of seamen pacing
with naked feet.

' I say,' says Captain Trollope, ' are you a
pretty strong crew here ? '

One man plucked a pipe from the

car that formed his mouth, and answered
' No.'

'Short-handed by how many?' asked Mr.
Davenire.

' By as many as we are,' answered the
other man.

' How's the salt beef in these parts?'
asked Captain Trollope, lighting a cigar.

' Ain't got to it yet. Had fresh messes so
far,' answered one of them.

' I have known a rotten harness cask,'
said Mr. Hankey, staring at the two men by
the moonlight betwixt his hard, black whiskers,
' breed the bloodiest mutiny that was ever
heard of at sea. I say, Davenire, think of
the spirit of murder lying pickled in a barrel
of beef! What romance-hunter would seek
for the fiend *there?* But I'll tell you what,'
said he, stepping up close to the two astonished seamen, ' when the sheath-knife's too
blunt to fashion a tobacco-jar, or even a comb
for a sweetheart, out of the beef that's served

to men to nourish them, and to give them
bone, heart, and hands for the halliards and
the handspike, why——' he broke off with a
theatrical laugh, and rounding on his heel
sauntered aft, watched by the brace of Jacks
till he was out of sight on the poop.

It was just about then that the chief mate,
who was in charge of the watch, uttered an
exclamation, and at the same moment a rocket
was distinctly observed to explode some considerable distance astern. A little later the
steady glare of a port-fire showed, and this was
followed by another and yet another rocket.

'That's from the little craft that was hanging astern this afternoon,' said the captain to
the mate.

'She must be signalling us, sir. There's
nothing else in sight.'

'What could she want with us? Has a
mail-bag been omitted? Another rocket!
Bring the ship to, sir, and let us see what's
wrong there.'

This was done amidst some excitement on the part of the passengers. Even now in these the first few hours of their departure from port, the monotony of the deep was felt. Here was to be a picture by moonlight—a pursuit all the way from Sydney Harbour, something more to look at and think of than the white splendour flowing to the bows.

'Aft here, my lads, and round in on the mainbraces! Put your helm a-starboard!'

And amidst some stamping, harmonised by song, the ship was brought to the wind, and Mrs. Peacock, who watched the movements of the men from the side of Mrs. Storr, on gazing up at the heavens, beheld with astonishment that the moon had changed her position.

A group of the male passengers stood together on the quarter, and after looking one another in the face by the bright light, talked softly.

'What can she be?' says the gentleman

named Davenire, staring with all his might into that part of the sea where the fireworks had shone.

'Chaw! nothing for us to trouble about,' said Mr. Shannon.

'Doocid odd though, all the same,' muttered Captain Trollope, 'just out from Sydney, and chased all the afternoon.'

'Any message for us, d'ye think?' softly exclaimed the handsome and decayed-looking Masters, strolling to the group.

'I'd be glad to see her sink if I thought so,' answered Captain Trollope.

Here another fellow with an air of aimlessness approached the knot of men which, had you then counted them, you would have found ten. On the other side of the deck where the skipper and mates stood were the rest of the passengers. Suddenly Captain Trollope, looking round, seemed sensible of the character and quality of the group he formed one of.

'Come, break up!' he whispered, and in a

moment the little company dissolved, some joining the ladies, others stepping the deck, others silently overhanging the rail.

Old Captain Benson raised and let fall the night-glass to and from his eye with a manner of strong impatience. He was not used to detention of this sort. He felt there was nothing distressful in the matter, and seemed to find something impudent in a signal that required him to stop. The night wind was gentle, full of dew; it blew perhaps a four-knot breeze, and the old skipper's heart yearned to brace it. The snow-white sails of the main curved stirless to the mast, and there was not swell enough in the ocean to flap as much as the noise of a hand-clap from the rest of the cloths.

The *Queen* must have lain like a beacon of light upon that sea for the stranger to steer for, and within twenty minutes of the ship having been hove-to there came floating to the vessel, shining like a fabric wrought out

of the lights of the deep, a large powerful
cutter, shredding the dark brine into gleams
and froth. Down came her great main-sail
with a roar of hoops, and whilst a strong
voice was shouting for an end of rope, the
clever little craft glided close in under the
counter where she lay with three or four men
in her, all looking up. The moonlight flashed
her white planks into ivory, and painted in
clear colours the figure of a man standing
near the mast with a portmanteau beside him.
A fellow, letting go the tiller, ran a few steps,
and shouted, looking aloft at the crowd of
faces upon the ship's quarter.

'Is Captain Benson there?'

'Ay,' said the captain slowly; 'what do
you want?'

'We've brought off a gent who wishes to
be put aboard.'

'Where is he?' said the captain.

'Here,' said the man, who stood beside the
portmanteau, advancing to the rail of the

cutter; 'I beg you will allow me to come on board.'

'But what do you want, sir?' shouted old Benson, glaring suspiciously down at the figure that was dressed in a black coat and light trousers and a soft dark hat; he was clearly no official.

'You will not ask me to call out my business from this low elevation, sir.'

After a pause:

'Throw a ladder over the side,' sang out Captain Benson.

The man seemed to shake hands with the fellow who had run from the tiller; some thought the gesture looked as though he gave him money. He gained the deck swiftly, clawing up the steps with one hand, whilst he held his portmanteau with the other. Captain Trollope passed him close humming; a few others brushed by him also in silence, and all whilst he stood for a few minutes on the deck fetching his breath.

But even in that time, whilst the captain, mates, and passengers were waiting for the stranger to approach, a fellow in the bows of the cutter let go the rope's end; you heard a halloing of some sailors' song as the gaff of the cutter's mainsail mounted, and to the astonishment of Captain Benson she was off, leaning from the breeze, fretting the silver under the counter into a wake, with the fellow at the helm brawling out, 'A good voyage to you!'

The mate stood a moment looking idly on, then sent a bull-like roar to the cutter to return and stand by the ship till it was seen what the passenger wanted. A growling 'No, no,' rolled back through the damp night breeze, and the cutter grew dim in the silver haze of the night.

By this time the new arrival, grasping his portmanteau, had walked aft to Captain Benson, vigilantly and distrustfully eyed by several of the male passengers as he went;

indeed, they followed him and hung close to catch what passed. You could almost read by the light of the moon; the stranger's figure and face were as determinable as by daylight; he was rather short and rather slim, and wore long whiskers of a pale yellow. He was very white, and his dark eyes glistened in their settings as he rolled them round upon the people.

'I do believe,' whispered Mr. Dent to his wife whilst he bobbed his head with intent eyes at the man, 'that he's James Murray.'

'Do you mean the manager of the such-and-such a bank?' said she, giving it its name.

By this time Captain Benson appeared to have recognised him.

'Why you're Mr. Murray, hain't ye?'

'That's my name, captain, and if you will step apart I'll give you my reason for desiring to sail in this ship to England, and my excuse for becoming a passenger in an irregular way.'

'What does he want to say?' muttered Captain Trollope to Mr. Davenire.

'Is one small portmanteau all his luggage for England?' answered the other.

'I think I recognise an acquaintance,' exclaimed Mr. Murray, and he extended his hand to Mr. Dent, lifting his hat at the same time to the colonial merchant's wife.

'Get way upon the ship, Mr. Matthews,' said Captain Benson, and with little courtesy or ceremony he said, 'Step below, sir.'

Mr. Murray, picking up his portmanteau, followed the white-haired skipper down the companion steps. Captain Trollope and one or two others lurked in a heedless off-hand way round about the open skylight, through which they were able to look straight down into the cuddy. But Captain Benson and Mr. Murray sat out of earshot at the head of the table where the captain's chair was. The old man fastened his deep-set searching eyes upon his companion, who was certainly pale and agitated; but then, to be sure, the situation he had placed himself in was an extraordinary one. He was a man of about forty, and pulling down one of his long yellow flowing whiskers, he spoke thus :—

'It was only at the last moment, Captain Benson, when, in short, it was too late to book a passage in your ship, that I received a letter from London requiring my immediate presence at our office there. It concerns some enormous piece of rascality, and I am the only one in the Australian employ who can help them.'

'When did you get this letter?' asked the captain.

'A ship from London arrived last night— what's her name again?'

'The *Magician*!' suggested the captain.

'So,' said Murray, 'if her mails were not late in delivery, at all events my letters did not come to hand until noon. Unfortunately I was out on business. When I returned to

the bank and read the commands from
London your ship had started, or was about
to start. I was determined to take the first
ship and a clipper, and immediately hired the
cutter *Wooloomooloo* to follow you, giving myself no time to bring off more luggage than
what you see there,' said he, pointing to his
portmanteau.

Captain Trollope and Mr. Davenire came
into the cuddy, and Trollope drank a glass of
water. Davenire carelessly hummed. They
looked searchingly and suspiciously at Murray
as they passed him, pausing on the steps as
though but to catch a single syllable.

'But all this is very irregular, Mr.
Murray,' said Captain Benson, whose formal
sea prejudices were working in him as though
they would rise to a passion. 'You could
have taken the next ship, sir.'

'But good heavens, captain,' cried Murray,
'you know very well what the detention has
been through desertion; a chance for sailing

from Sydney may not happen for another month.'

The skipper's mahogany countenance relaxed, for this was the truth, as he knew, and it was a good excuse too.

'Of course, sir, I pay you your passage money all the same, as though I had booked at your agent's,' continued Murray, pulling out a note-book well lined with sovereigns and Bank of England notes. 'The matter is extraordinary, the case quite exceptional. You shall hear all of it as we go along,' he continued, pouring out his words with an oily fluency, under which the captain's temper was entirely unable to break. 'Any cabin forward or aft will do for me, and, of course, I pay first-class fare. Can I have something to eat now, sir? I am starving.'

The passengers were beginning to leave the deck when the captain rose. He called to the steward, and surlily bade him find Mr. Murray a bed, and provide him with some refreshments : then went on deck. It was five bells—half-past ten. The passengers had hung about above, unwilling to intrude, but they had come to want their grog and biscuits at last, and some of them were sleepy.

'A strange business this,' said Mr. Dent, meeting the captain at the head of the companion steps. 'What brings Murray away in such a hurry?'

Mr. Caldwell and Mr. Shannon, who stood by, lounged a little closer. The captain briefly gave the colonial merchant Murray's story in effect.

'Wouldn't the chasing of a clipper ship in a cutter be considered a rather lunatic scheme?' exclaimed the black-faced Mr. Caldwell, joining in. 'Why, in anything of a breeze this ship would be twenty parallels ahead of that cutter in a week.'

'True, sir, I don't understand it,' answered the captain, and he slipped from the little knot of people and walked to the wheel, near

E 2

which stood the mate. Mr. Matthews was
moving forwards, for wherever the captain
takes his stand there the deck is sacred :—

'Within that circle none durst walk but he.'

But the skipper softly hailed the worthy
fellow, and he returned.

Oh, what a glorious Pacific night was that
through which the ship was then sailing!
The captain and mate stood aft, the ink-black
shadow of the helmsman swayed slowly with
the play of a pendulum over the grating he
stood on ; the planks of pearl ran forward
vacant, save that a couple of figures talked
together at the port extremity of the poop sunk
in shadow there. The ship shone with light,
and was as fair to see as a meteor of the skies
as she rippled along her course, leaving a
luminous dust-like wake behind her.

'What was the next ship for England?'
said the captain.

The mate named her.

' Was she well forward ? '

' She only wanted men.'

'After all,' said the captain, looking astern, ' foreseeing the weather, and guessing our distance, Murray showed smartness in capturing us as he has. They should reward him at home for his promptness. How many bank managers would have exhibited this activity ? '

' I've never seen him before,' said the plain-spoken mate, ' and I don't like his looks.'

'He showed money in plenty for his passage. A passenger's looks no more concern a ship than the cut and colour of her figure-head. He arrived starved and frightened, sir.'

'With a little portmanteau for a long voyage, sir,' said the mate.

The captain grunted. The mate certainly sometimes exhibited an unreasonable dulness of mind. Mr. Matthews was again about to move forward.

'Have you any acquaintance amongst the passengers, sir?'

The white-haired skipper was of the old school, and sir'd a man with the pomp and persistency of old Sam himself.

'No, sir,' answered the mate; 'I believe Mr. Poole knows one or two of them.'

The captain made a step to the skylight, looked down and watched for a moment in silence those of the passengers whose figures he could compass, as they sat at table sipping and munching. They included one or two ladies, and Captain Henry Trollope showed in bold relief, and so too did Mr. Masters and Mr. Burn, who was drinking bottled beer. Sounds of laughter and talk arose. The captain made another step, and caught sight of Mr. Murray squaring his elbows at a tray of refreshments and talking eagerly to Mr. Dent. He returned to the mate who awaited him.

'Some of our gentlemen passengers,' said he, 'appear to have seen hard times.'

' And hard drinking, sir.'

' The goldfields soon toughen a man into rough looks, they say,' said the captain. ' A few of them appear as though they knew the ropes. I caught one casting as sailorly an eye as ever a seaman directed at the set of the ship's sails.'

He paused, and then made some reference to the ship's course and the promise of the weather, and went below, leaving the mate to trudge out his solitary watch till midnight.

CHAPTER III

THE BANK MANAGER

NEXT morning the wind was off the bow—a head wind—and the seas ridging at the ship in rich, sparkling lines of violet and lace. When the passengers came on deck after breakfast they found the second mate, who had charge of the ship, standing at the rail with his arm round a backstay, gazing with the idle eyes of custom at the large figure of a whale that was swelling wet, black and gleaming, along the course of the ship, half a mile away to windward.

It was a fine sight when the huge, gleaming bulk rose and fell with the motions of a ship, bursting the glittering heads of brine into snowstorms, whilst, as though it pulsed its way along with a steam-engine inside, it blew a tall spout which arched like a feather when the weight of the wind took it.

Mr. Hankey stepped halfway up the poop ladder with a pipe in his mouth, and said to the second mate, who stood just above, close by :

' Do you see yonder cloud that's almost in shape of a camel ? '

' By the mass, and 'tis like a camel indeed,' answered Poole, grinning.

' Methinks it is like a weasel,' said Mr. Hankey.

' It is backed like a weasel,' exclaimed the second mate, laughing heartily.

' Or like a whale,' cried Mr. Hankey.

' Very like a whale,' answered the second mate, with the tears standing in his eyes.

Mr. Hankey nodded his appreciation ; probably this was the only second mate then afloat who could have Poloniused him so aptly and quick. He raised his foot by another step to command with his eye the platform of the poop, and said:

'Did you ever hear of a man chasing a clipper to get a passage?'

'There are plenty of instances of belated passengers overtaking vessels in small boats and otherwise,' answered the second mate, looking aft to see if the captain was on deck.

'What would the cutter charge for such a job?'

'A hundred sovereigns, every penny, and perhaps a heavy consideration on top if the chase was successful.'

'All for what?' said Mr. Hankey, looking at Mr. Murray, who stood alone right aft, staring at the whale.

'Ha!' said the second mate.

'And one little portmanteau,' said Mr. Hankey.

'Oh, that would be nothing, sir, when a man's in a hurry.'

'Do you smell anything like a rat?' said Mr. Hankey.

The second mate's grin instantly disappeared on his catching sight of the captain. He stepped aft, backwards, as though to command a clearer view of the main-royal, and Hankey, seating himself at the foot of the ladder, was joined in a very short time by Captain Trollope, Davenire, Burn, and Masters. There was a uniformity in the variety of this group of smokers that impressed the eye of even the second mate, when, having satisfied himself that the main-royal was properly set, he returned to his place at the head of the poop-ladder. He had known Mr. Hankey merely as a passenger when outward bound, and in Sydney had partaken of some friendly drinks with him. He had understood that his uncle was a lord in Holy Orders, and undoubtedly Mr. Hankey was a gentleman. Yet what was it, he thought, that made that knot of fellows beneath him so various in

their attire—alike, and yet unlike? Scarcely
their military bearing, though they had *that*,
some of them. He was puzzled, and scratched
the back of his head and looked right aft over
the stern at the lovely, delicately troubled
blue of the sea there; but once looking, he
continued to look, then to frown, then to
strain his sight. Muttering to himself ' By
Gosh ! ' he walked aft, touching his cap to
the captain, whom he thus addressed :

' There's a steamer's smoke right astern
of us, sir.'

The captain sheltered his eyes with his
hand.

' I believe I see it, sir,' said he, and looked
at the faint blue film through a telescope.

The second mate walked forward.

' What's the old man looking at ? ' said
Captain Trollope, rising to the height of the
ladder, and addressing Mr. Poole.

' There's a steamer coming up astern,'
answered the second mate shortly. His duty

as an officer in charge forbade him from conversing with the passengers. Captain Trollope descended the ladder in quick recoil, and
said in a hoarse, low, eager voice : ' There's a
steamer coming after us,' on which every man
knocked his pipe out and went on to the
poop.

A steamer in the days this story belongs
to was a real curiosity in those seas. A man-
of-war with a funnel might now and again be
met, sometimes with a foreign colour at her
mizzen-gaff : a few, but a very few, steamers
communicated between Europe and the Aus-
tralias. Hence the apparition of that smoke
lifting its fibrous height higher and yet higher
above the blue sea-limit, caused great excitement fore and aft. A steamer it certainly
was—not the smoke of a burning ship, as
Mr. Murray suggested, ' because, sir,' said the
captain, looking at his pale face and yellow
whiskers keenly and doubtfully, as though his
old-fashioned prejudices still viewed him as

an intruder, despite the fifty guineas the man had that morning put down, 'burning ships lie still, and yonder smoke is overtaking us.'

' What vessel *can* she be, do you think ? ' said Mr. Dent. 'There was no steamer at Sydney when we left.'

' Except the tug,' said Mr. Burn, who had pressed forward, speaking with a strong beery accent after a breakfast of bottled ale.

There was a general laugh. The notion of a tug being all this distance from her port was unusually rich and original.

The clipper broke her way somewhat sluggishly through the flowing lines of head sea, fiery with sunshine. She was off her course, half the main-royal was aback, and every weather-leech lifted at each light plunge of the bow. Her pace, therefore, was comparatively small, and as the breezes of the night had for the most part been faint and fluctuating, the distance she had already made from Sydney was not great. It was a noble, inspiriting morning ; the wind was of a rare softness, charged with some aroma of ocean, which might have come sweet with remoteness from the giant kelp of the Antarctic circle. An awning shaded the poop. The Jacks forward filled the eye with the various business of their vocation ; the main-deck ran from the quarter-deck white and clear ; the *Queen* carried no steerage passengers. From time to time a cow lowed in its stall ; hens cackled and pigs grunted. It was hot. Who could realise the ice and blackness of that Horn which the ship was by-and-by to pass, in the face of the trembling bed of light through which she was bruising her way ?

Extraordinary interest was manifested in the smoke astern by many of the gentlemen passengers. They did not trouble the captain with questions, but talked apart. Mr. Murray, on the other hand, had been a little importunate till the captain gave his arm to a lady and marched away. He had wanted to know if she was likely to prove a steamer from any other Australian port than Sydney, or was she a man-of-war? Was it conceivable that she was bringing more passengers for the clipper? He looked anxious and about ten years older than when at breakfast. Captain Trollope, Davenire, and one or two others of the set viewed him curiously.

'I don't think,' says Trollope to Caldwell in a low mysterious voice, 'that he'd fire a magazine as an alternative.'

'We keep too near the cust country,' exclaimed Mr. Hankey, looking at the smoke. 'I dare say some point of it is still in sight from the masthead.'

'Gentlemen,' said Mr. Storr, joining them, rubbing his hands, 'this, I think, promises to be a voyage of excitements.'

'What took you to Australia, sir?' said Captain Trollope, looking down at the little man over his big moustache.

'Business,' answered the auctioneer.

'Did pretty well, I hope?' said Mr. Masters.

'I did not dig for gold,' answered Mr. Storr, with a sarcastic glance of suspicion at the handsome but decayed young fellow.

'And so you *did* pretty well,' said Captain Trollope. 'Ha, ha! That's sheer betwixt the ribs of some of us, Hankey.'

Here Mr. Burn diverted the attention by arriving with Miss Mansel and the ship's telescope. The gentlemen crowded about the good-looking young woman to point the glass for her, and Mr. Masters begged her not to shut the eye which she applied to the tube. By this time the steamer had risen to the height of her paddle-boxes, disclosing a lean, dog's-eared funnel that vomited a black fat coil of smoke twenty miles long, and one pole mast forward, on which some signals were seen to be flying, but as the colours blew fore and aft they could not be distinguished. There was no doubt now that her business was with

the clipper. Indeed, Mr. Dent, after looking
at her through the telescope, professed to
recognise her as the tug *Bungaree*, of Sydney.
A mirage lifted her, and she looked closer
than she was. But she was splashing after
the ship at eight knots, and the clipper was
barely doing five, and presently she was showing her small squab hull fair upon the water
with the figures of men visible on the bridge,
and flags still streaming at the pole mast, but
dumb as a sea-tongue through being on end.

Captain Trollope looked for Mr. Murray ;
he had disappeared.

The barque was luffed till way was almost
shaken out of her. It was a moment of great
excitement. The chase of the cutter had been
nothing compared with it. Thrice in twenty-
four hours to be pursued! Old Benson was
puzzled. The traditions of the ocean seemed
all awry. Three weeks' detention in Sydney
Harbour through desertion! And, now, when
fairly away to be checked by a species of

pursuit unprecedented in his experience! However, it was clear enough the steamer wanted the ship. The second mate had managed to spell out the flags which, in Marryatt's Code, signified 'Important, must communicate.'

'Bring the ship to the wind, sir,' said Captain Benson to the officer.

She was a small clinker-built boat, with green. paddle-boxes, and the foam fled from her sponsons as the foot of a cataract hurls into its channel. Three men stood on her bridge, and as she came alongside with a beat of paddles that, with the arrest of the wheels, sank into a sullen roar of water, a man in a white wide-awake and long lean yellow face and linen jacket, hailed from the bridge.

'Ho, the *Queen* ahoy!'

'Hallo!' sang out Captain Benson.

'Has e'er a stranger been put aboard your ship since yer sailed from Sydney?'

'Yes, sir,' shouted back Captain Benson.

'Was he put aboard by the cutter *Wooloo-mooloo*?'

The captain lifted his hand.

'You must allow me to come on board if you please,' exclaimed one of the men who stood upon the bridge: he was dressed in a sort of uniform, a bell-shaped cap with naval peak, light cloth braided jacket of military cut. The captain of the steamer shouted down her call pipe: the paddles were manœuvred, the tug drew close alongside, and watching their opportunity as the slight swell rolled the two vessels to and from each other, the official-looking individual and another sprang on the barque and came aft.

'Good gracious me!' exclaimed Mrs. Dent to her husband, 'it's Superintendent Fox.'

The other might have passed for a Bow Street runner. His nose was like the end of a bludgeon, the left eye was twice the size of the right, and as he stepped aft with the superintendent he gazed with a grin of ragged black teeth round upon the people. Yet he was some sort of official too, to judge by his clothes. The superintendent walked right up to Captain Benson, and said quite audibly :

'You are the master of this ship, sir?'

'That's so,' answered the captain, puffing and straddling, and firmly settling his tall hat.

'I am here,' said the other, 'to arrest Mr. James Murray, manager of the such-and-such a bank, Sydney, for embezzlement.'

'Lor !' said the captain, 'what's the amount, sir?'

'Seventy-six thousand pounds.'

Captain Trollope whistled long and low. The fellow with the horrible grin of teeth turned slowly and looked at him.

'It seems as if others are to have the innings,' said Mr. Caldwell, in a hoarse whisper in the ear of Mr. Cavendish, who was staring with his congenital grin, made loathsome through the projection of his upper lip by his eye teeth.

'I don't see my man,' said the superintendent, running his eyes over the group of passengers, following on with a level, penetrating
stare at the seamen forwards who had struck
work for the moment to gaze aft.

'Go and tell Mr. Murray he is wanted, sir,'
said Captain Benson to the second mate, who,
knowing where to look, ran down the companion steps : he was instantly followed by the
superintendent and his assistant.

Captain Benson remained on deck. The
passengers talked in whispers. The sensation
was profound. Mr. Mark Davenire and another
went stealthily to the skylight and peered
down : their ears seemed to enlarge as they
strained them. It was about eleven o'clock
in the morning. The sun was shining with a
strong heat, and there was a sense as of being
in harbour with that tug lying close alongside
panting in her heart : the blue water slopped
noisily between the two vessels as they rolled
at each other, and Mr. Burn, leaning over the

rail, seemed able to forget what was going forward in the ship in laughing at the tug's helmsman, whose thin shape shot out of a pair of compasses into a mere pellet of head, a mere rope of onions, the littlest on top.

'This state of suspense is dreadful,' whispered Miss Mansel to Mr. Shannon. 'What will they do to the wretched man?'

'Put him in chains,' answered the ship's surgeon, who stood near.

'The brutality of it!' exclaimed Mr. Shannon, with a face that was suddenly dark with passion. 'Did you ever see a chain gang?'

The girl with a shudder answered that she had seen men on railway platforms in England linked together, and that had been a sight that sickened her. Mr. Shannon was about to speak when he caught a look from Captain Trollope; it was a look of menace, almost of fury; it had but the life of an instant; next breath the tall soldierly-looking

man seemed to be listening at the companion-
way at what was passing below.

All on a sudden up rushed Poole, the
second mate.

'Where's the doctor?' he shouted.

'Here,' answered the ship's surgeon.

'You're wanted, sir!'

The surgeon ran after the mate into the
cuddy. The captain's teak-coloured face betwixt its fringe of white hairs took a resolved
hard weather look; he walked apart from
the passengers, and strode in short excursions
beside the wheel, guessing a fatality and
awaiting its report.

What was the doctor wanted for? the
passengers wondered. Had Murray stabbed
himself, shot himself? No; they'd have
heard the report of a pistol in that scene of
deck subdued by alarm and expectation,
whilst on high all was still, but for now and
again the gull-like cry of a suddenly jerked
block.

Mr. Storr, standing beside the companion hatch, faintly cried, 'Good God!' and made a quick step out of the way. In fact the companion ladder was then full of figures rising clumsily with the dead weight of a man's body. There was a general recoil, and most of the ladies went hurriedly forward.

'By Jove, he's killed himself!' said Mr. Davenire.

The rest of his friends looked on with cold faces.

The lifeless body of Mr. James Murray was passed through the companion-hatch in the triple clutch of the hideous rogue of the black teeth, the superintendent, and the second mate. They put it flat down upon the deck, right in the way of a ray of sunshine that flooded the convulsed face, which looked alive with the movement of the muscles. The surgeon dropped a large silk handkerchief over the dreadful countenance.

'Is it a fit, sir?' exclaimed Captain

Benson, coming along smartly on his rounded shanks from his sacred walk near the wheel, both his loose arms jerking with agitation and temper.

'Poison, sir,' said the surgeon.

'He was too quick for us,' said the superintendent, with a surly look at the corpse.

'Did he poison himself?' cried the captain, who unconsciously formed the centre of a crescent of passengers, with one very white face under Mr. Storr's straw hat.

The superintendent whispered to his ugly mate, who rolled below, and returned with the dead man's portmanteau.

'He had come prepared,' said the surgeon to the captain.

'But with what?' demanded the skipper.

'Prussic acid.'

'A surer trick than the bullet,' whispered Hankey to Masters.

'It makes no mess, certainly,' said Masters,

looking as coolly at the body as if it had been a fish newly landed.

'Do you carry it back with you?' said the captain.

'Ay, sir, yes, along with that,' replied the superintendent, pointing to the portmanteau.

'Then for God's sake,' cried the old skipper with an angry toss of both his fins, 'take 'em both out of the ship at once, sir; take 'em both out of the ship at once, and leave us to proceed. Is that a sight for ladies?'

' I should be obliged by a sailor or two to help,' said the superintendent.

They contrived it by placing the body on a grating covered with a piece of sailcloth, that the ladies who lingered on deck might not continue to be shocked. They passed the dead wretch through the gangway, and, watching their chance, cleverly launched grating and figure to the paddle-box of the steamer, where the thing was caught, the body removed, and the grating returned.

'Is it all right with you?' sang out the captain.

'All right, sir,' answered the master of the tug. But no hand was flourished, no signal of farewell exchanged. It had been too ugly a business to admit of any sort of kindness.

'Only this very morning at breakfast,' said Mrs. Peacock, with a working face to Mrs. Storr, 'he was talking to me most affably. He knew my husband well. I find it impossible to think of him as a villain.'

'I find it harder to think of him at all,' answered Mrs. Storr. 'Only imagine! he was talking to me and my husband this morning about his intention of settling in London, and of buying a house through Mr. Storr. His voice trembles upon my ear still. It is now the voice of a ghost. I am thankful the sun is up.'

'Trim sail,' cried the captain. 'Round with that maintop-sail smartly, Mr. Poole.'

His command was re-echoed by the second mate with the voice of a young lion. In a minute the poop rang with the yeo-ho heave-hoing of pulling and hauling Jacks. The tug splashed her paddles heavily alongside, floated ahead, and curved away for Sydney. The sun sparkled in splendour in her broad race of foam, and the light sea tossed it, and the bright breeze whipped it into many glittering fragments of rainbow, till it looked like a stretch of flower garden in tow of her. The breeze had freshened on a sudden without shifting its quarter or blowing up a rag of cloud; when sail was trimmed the clipper took the brilliant gushing of wind as a horse starts to the touch of its rider. She heeled her three shining spires with their flights of steady wings between; the sea-flash broke in smoke from her weather bow. The white water swept in a smooth, silky seething alongside.

'He paid his passage-money, too,' mused the old skipper, pausing at the companion-hatch, with his deep-set eyes fixed upon the receding figure of the tug. 'A cheaply earned fifty guineas, and not his to spend either. So, I suppose——'

Here the old chap gave a start, remembering the time, and a few minutes later he had returned on deck, and was screwing the sun down to the sea, with an occasional glance, in the intervals of his observation, at the line of smoke astern, and a look once or twice at Captain Trollope and some others, who stood in a knot at the lee-mizzen rigging deep in conversation that hummed with wary undertones.

CHAPTER IV

THE SLEEP-TALKER

THEY talked over this matter of embezzlement
and suicide in the forecastle as well as in the
cabin. Were you ever in a ship's forecastle?
Did you *never* see a company of sailors dining
in their sea parlour?

Here is an interior with a little square
hole for light and escape called a scuttle; you
may also enter it by way of the main-deck,
round the windlass ends. Nearly all hands
are below: the kids full of smoking meat
have been brought along from the galley, and
the sailors are falling to. What a fall to is
that! No table, no chairs, no convenience of
any sort. Hammocks bulge in grimy bulk
from the ceilings; a few bunks are shaped to

the ship's side, and vanish in the darkness of
' the eyes' right forward. There is not light
enough to see by, although it is noon by the
captain's sextant. So Jack has lighted his
flare of wick and slush, which confounds the
vision in the recess by a dance of shadows.

The men still feed upon fresh meat, Australian mutton at threehalfpence a pound,
mangled remains of beef which, whilst yoked
to the wool waggon, was wrought by five
hundred leagues of travel into black veins
and muscle tough as the upland spruce.

Jack sits upon his chest, or in his bunk.
He has jobbed at the contents of the mess
kid, and having got his whack gone away
with it like a dog. You may see him sawing
at a cube of bullock's heart with the tarry
blade he carries for shipboard work in his
sheath, munching sullenly like an old goat,
with a curse at the leather betwixt his teeth,
whilst he balances his pannikin to the light,
watching the black rum and water sway as

though he expected some revelation of tadpole. He is happy at last when he flings tin plate and tin pannikin down, and pulling out a plug of tobacco leisurely cuts himself a pipeful.

'I say, mates,' sings out Bill, lighting his pipe with a ropeyarn at the lamp, 'how do a man feel when he's pisoned?'

'As I do,' says Joe. 'They spits better meat than this in London town for cats. Why don't they send cat's meat to sea? It's nothen but dawg's meat for sailors, I allow.'

'I helped to tilt the poor devil on to the grating,' said one of the men, 'and I'm bubbled if you couldn't feel him a stiffening just as with the eye ye see a piece of wood a-curling when it's on fire.'

'Git out,' said a sulky sailor called Jim.

'S'elp me then, you old cuckoo, but I ought to know, for I 'ad the 'andling of him.'

'How much did 'e steal?' asked a sailor.

'Why,' answered Tom gravely, as one who

is acquainted with the meaning of figures, 'I
hear it was a matter of about a quarter of a
million.'

Silence. No man had any notion of that
quantity, and none liked to expose his
ignorance.

'When I first caught sight of that chap,'
continued Tom, 'I guessed there was something up. I don't like a man who wears long
whiskeys. I once sailed with a man with long
whiskeys, and he tried to put his ship ashore
twice whilst I was on board. He managed it
arter I left her. When I caught sight of him
this morning, I says to myself, thinks I, if
you're going to sail along with us, thinks I,
stand by, my livelies, for a voyage of blue
moons. Why,' he continued, extending his
hand, 'his chasing of us showed him up.
Why didn't he ship like the others? But he
was of that sort, I allow, who reckons that a
man's nakedness can be hidden by his tarring
himself all over.'

'What did he take that killed him?' asked a man.

Nobody knew.

'Reckon it stowed snugly and might be worth a man's carrying about,' continued the sailor. 'Think of an open boat like what we passed yesterday: throat so scorched that when ye mutter for a drink, ye start and look round wondering what devil in the air was mocking of ye. Wouldn't the little portable, whatever it was, that saved that man from chains and the lash, come in middling handy at such a time?'

The speaker resumed his pipe and gazed around to observe the effect produced by his powerful imagination.

'I wish that old owl 'ud belay his jaw. He's too gallus quick with his blue lights,' sang out a querulous voice from a hammock.

'I'll tell you what,' exclaimed the man Tom in a mysterious voice, whilst the atmo-sphere of slush-flare and dim daylight turned of a faint blue with tobacco smoke; 'that there covey as was took off ain't the only rumdiddles aboard this ship.'

None of the men seemed much interested.

A voice under the scuttle exclaimed, 'There's a cove aboard this ship with a face ate up by drink. He looks as decayed as an old cheese, as the jagged side of the moon in a telescope. I've some recollection of having met that man. I've some recollection,' continued the voice, 'of a man having been stabbed to the heart in a quarrel, and of a chap all the same as this pocky party being wanted for the job.'

'There's more'n one of them first-class passengers,' says Bill, 'who's been to sea. I'll swear to that; though they mayn't have the looks they've got the eyes of sailors.'

'Sogers you swear. Don't talk of 'em as sailors,' exclaimed Tom. 'I make out ten. There's a sort of professional likeness among 'em, though you shall tell me one bunker stands six foot with a mustachy, whilst another might be a forecastle duff on end. I know I ain't to be mistook. I've been along with troops afore now, and I can tell ye a military officer without asking for his sword ' (spit).

'Two or three came for'rads yesterday,' exclaimed a fellow grinning so hard that he was forced to pull a sooty inch of pipe from betwixt his teeth, 'and was for working up a mutiny, durn me, ha! ha! Talk of the harness cask and the demon of murder a-lying in it. If the mate overhears you, thinks I! he whips off on his heels just as though he'd been saying nothing of consequence. But I'll tell ye what, there's more powder for bust-ups in them half-laughs and purser's grins than in the straight-faced tip.'

Here they were interrupted by a roaring voice in the scuttle. Pipes were emptied, caps adjusted, and half the men tumbled out into the sunshine to go on with the work of the ship.

The horizon was clear, but the slant of the vessel was sharp with freshening gusts, and in one of them, as it swept salt blue and shrill over the bulwark rail, splitting into railway whistles upon the shrouds, the mate of the watch bawled out an order for the fore and mizzen royals to be clewed up, and the flying jib to be hauled down. A misty appearance thickened the blue on the weather bow, and some stuff like scud, pale as though whitened by moonlight, was flying up out of it.

'In main-royal and gaff-topsail,' called out the skipper from the weather quarter.

The barque was thrashing through it nobly then. The froth lifted pouring in swells or humps of dazzling whiteness from either quarter; and the sea-smoke flew like explosions of cannon from the bow. The awning was rattling like the feather in Miss Mansel's hat.

'We must have the mainsail off her.'

The men raced with a will to the summons

of the mate's voice. High aloft the main-royal was ballooning from the grip of its gear. A man was hauling taut on its lee brace when Mr. Davenire, standing clear of the ridge-rope of the awning, close beside the main-rigging, and staring on high, exclaimed to Mr. Alexander Burn :

' I think we might manage it.'

' Off, ye lendings ! ' cried Burn.

The two men whipped off their coats in a jiffy and were halfway up the rigging, whilst the sailors were still busy with the gear belonging to the sail.

'What did I tell ye?' says Bill in the waist, looking up.

' A fine mess they'll make of it,' was the answer. ' All to be done over again.'

The two gentlemen reaching the futtock rigging, gained the top with wonderfully nimble knees. Fat as he was, Mr. Burn did not stop to blow. On the contrary, he showed the road, and was shinning up the topgallant rigging when Davenire was making a breathless pause of it for a moment or two in the cross-trees.

Old Captain Benson, gripping the weather-vang, looked up with a face of stern disapproval, which slowly softened, however, when he saw the sail swiftly fining down into lines of man-of-war-like neatness and a very daisy of a bunt. He was astonished. Mr. Burn, coming into the cross-trees, gazed down with a flourish of his hand.

'Main topgallants'l, sir?' he sung down.

'No, no, gentlemen, not yet, thank 'ee,' cried the mate, laughing and looking aft at the captain.

'I'll warrant that sail to go round the Horn without blowing adrift,' says Mr. Burn, in his wheezy, frothy, bottled-beer voice, to the mate as he stepped out of the rigging and put on his coat.

Captain Trollope, lounging to leeward, muttered to one of his friends as the hearty figure of Burn went along the weather side of the poop to court the congratulations of the captain.

'I wish those fools wouldn't show off. Burn bubbles over with self-conceit. He froths, like his ale, with it. If there were no women on board, Burn would keep quiet.'

'He talks in his sleep,' answered the other, who was Mr. Isaac Cavendish, the man with the little eyes, and odious, self-complacent grin. 'I heard a voice in his cabin last night. It was Burn's—a jolly silly voice, a beery babble.'

'If that's so, he must shift,' said Captain Trollope rapidly, frowning as he again sent a glance at Burn. 'Let's go below and see if it can be managed.'

Meanwhile, Burn, turning a hot and grinning countenance upon the passengers as he walked, stepped up to old Benson, and said, 'Well, captain, what do you think of that for a stow?'

'Sir,' answered the captain, with some blood of confusion, and perhaps of temper, deepening with a new shade the heavy weather stains upon his face, 'it is a very good stow, I have no doubt, but aboard my ship it is not customary for the passengers to do the work of the sailors.'

'Not the dirty work, naturally,' said Burn, half closing one eye as he turned his gaze upon the man at the wheel. 'But a little clean, healthful gymnastics, you know—besides you're short-handed, I believe.'

'We shall be able to manage, sir,' replied the captain, bridling.

'Didn't it make you sick to look down?' said Mr. Storr, who had stealthily paced up to listen.

'No; but was it because I didn't see you?' exclaimed Burn, bursting into a shout of laughter and catching hold of the astonished auctioneer by the arm. 'Only a joke, my dear fellow. Sick! Why,' says he, talking loud that all might hear, 'it's like going to heaven to be up there; you can hear the angels singing. Is there a musician amongst us able to bestride a yard-arm with a note-book and take down the melodies of the skies?'

Old Captain Benson walked forward on indignant legs to get out of the way. Though he reckoned that this spouter might have been once a seaman, he guessed by his looks and speech he was now fresh from the stage, a profession he despised through ignorance of the many affecting qualities of the actor.

The barque stormed along; the mainsail was off her, but she could bear the rest, and her hull swept phantom-like in a shadowing of spray; the bow seas smote her, and she leapt them with living grace. She was off her course, however, by three points, and this kept old Benson looking to windward. There was nothing more to come, however, in the shape of wind, spite of the blue dimness and the rags of steam-like stuff blowing out of it. Indeed, before the afternoon had far advanced the breeze had scanted, had shifted into the southward, and when the passengers went below to dinner they left the ship clothed to her trucks as in the morning, the yards slightly braced in, and the watch rigging out the fore-topmast studding sail boom.

It was a quiet dinner-party that evening; the suicide that day, the shock of it—for Murray had been well known to several—worked on the ladies. The captain talked in quiet tones to Mr. Dent and Mr. Storr. He seemed not to desire the conversation of the others or to evade it; he was civil, but his behaviour was that of a man who doesn't know his company. Some must have noticed this, but they allowed it to make no visible impression. They found the mate at the foot disposed to be chatty, and their talk was principally occupied with such texts as he provided or they suggested.

This was strange, you would have thought; as they had many experiences in common, and could have found themselves perfectly independent of mate or skipper. At intervals one would speak of the goldfields; another, perhaps, would let fall something dreamy and confused about the bush (the worst culprit in this special knowledge was Mr. Patrick Weston, whose face had a strange twisted look, as though famine having wrung it, conscience had fixed it, defying all after days of better cheer to help it). But on the whole their chat betrayed little or nothing of themselves or their past. Some seemed to have tried their luck on the stage, and the whole of the ten seemed to know a great deal about ships and the sea. If, indeed, they were boldly questioned, they made answer. Miss Mansel, for instance, who sat opposite to the great figure of Mark Davenire, said that she wondered he had had courage to climb the mast. Was he ever a sailor?

'Why, yes,' he answered, rolling in his chair as he clutched at the swing tray for a decanter of Marsala, 'when a boy I was a sailor. All good boys go to sea.'

'And you remember how to stow a sail after all these years, sir?' says the mate.

'I'll tell you what, Mr. Matthews,' exclaimed Davenire, poising a full glass, 'I believe you could put me to no job aboard this ship which you wouldn't find me superior to.'

'One would think, gentlemen,' said the mate, lying back in his chair and talking softly—he did not choose that the captain should think him too fluent—'that some of you had shipped in anticipation of finding the vessel short-handed.'

This was awkwardly put and meant. It was taken in ill part, and the men fell to talking one to another across the table in light off-hand speeches about the wind and the weather, giving no heed to the mate, who presently rose with something of a look of chagrin, and marched on deck to watch the ship.

The darkness drew round in as gentle and lovely a night as that which had preceded it : the moonlight flooded the zenith, and the spires of the *Queen* shot straight up into the silver air, every cloth silent with the breathing of the soft night wind. But by eleven o'clock the cabin lamps, saving one faint glimmer, were extinguished ; old Benson had gone to his cabin, the passengers had turned in ; the second mate walked in lonely watch, and the man at the wheel rose and fell in a shape of bronze tinctured with the gleam of the binnacle lamp.

Seven bells had been struck, when a tall radish of a figure came out of one of the cabins, and, going round the foot of the table, entered, without ceremony, a berth that immediately faced it. Two gentlemen occupied this berth. The tall figure was Mr. Isaac

Cavendish; he laid his hand upon the man in the upper bed, who violently started up with a most significant swift motion of his arm to his pillow. The light of the moon was upon the sea, and the sheen of it filled the berth with a delicate mist.

'Trollope, I want you to come and hear Burn talking in his sleep,' says Cavendish in a whisper. 'You may hear him *here!*'

The gentleman who occupied the under berth was Patrick Weston: he was snoring dismally just then in gulps and gasps like a pump when it sucks. Yet despite the clamour raised by those bellows of nostrils, the two gentlemen could distinctly hear a noisy voice proceeding from a cabin abreast—a greasy voice that sometimes attempted a tragic note which it cut short with a laugh. In silence Captain Trollope sprang out of his bunk. He was attired, as his companion was, for his bed, presentable for an emergency, such as fire or collision. They crossed the cuddy and

entered Mr. Cavendish's berth, which he
shared with Mr. Caldwell. This gentleman
lay a very corpse in sleep, thanks to a
draught which the surgeon had given him for
a face-ache.

Trollope and Cavendish closed the door
and listened. Their motive was to discover
if Burn's words penetrated the bulkhead.
Cavendish insisted that he had caught some
syllables. They now stood with straining
ears. It generally happens that when you
are prepared to listen the noise ceases—that
when you have run to bring your friend to
witness an object it has disappeared. They
had to wait ten minutes before Burn was
again disturbed by a dream. He then an-
nounced his intention to begin by an odd
parrot-like laugh.

'Hush!' whispered Trollope; 'even that
noise is enough to bring the captain out upon
him.'

'No use in attempting Othello here,' spoke

the dreamer with a distinctness of utterance
that was highly alarming to those whose ears
were in waiting. 'What do you say? . . . I
wish you wouldn't be so infernally imperti-
nent. What's that again? . . .' Here came a
long pause as though he gave his phantom
opponent plenty of time to explain himself.
He then began to mutter. The tone was
derisive, the words inaudible.

'We had better make him understand at
once that this won't do,' whispered Trollope;
and they passed into Mr. Burn's berth.

It was the smallest berth in the ship—a
mere hole, with a bull's-eye for a window.
It contained but one bunk, and in it the two
men dimly distinguished the lumpish figure
of Mr. Burn, with one leg over the edge of
his bed, in a posture of conviviality. His
right arm was mad with pantomime, and he
muttered in a low tragedy note in blank
verse. Captain Trollope watched him, then
let his hand fall upon his shoulder. Burn

instantly started up with a horrid ringing scream. It is told of a certain Scotchman that he delivered a yell like a wolf on stepping out of a bathing machine and putting his foot into the water. Such another cry did this man Burn raise as he sprang out of his bed, and, half asleep as he was, contorted his half-clad shape of suet into a fighting attitude.

The cry aroused everybody. Cabin doors were opened, and questions in male and female voices were hissed through the cuddy. The captain, in a long pea-coat scarcely concealing the extremities of a pair of bed-drawers, came out of his cabin and hastily turned up the lamp. He shouted to the mate through the open skylight to know what horrible cry was that; and the mate, putting his head into the open frame, replied that he had heard no cry, and didn't know what the captain meant.

'It's only Mr. Burn, who howled in his

sleep. It's all right! he's awake now,' said Captain Trollope, making a step into the cuddy.

The captain bowled down to Mr. Burn's door to satisfy himself; then, growling out 'Glad it isn't murder, sir,' went on deck to look at the ship and the night, whilst most of the passengers returned to their beds. Two or three, however, came gliding round the table to Burn's cabin.

'What the deuce is wrong?' whispered one.

'Go to your cabin, Hankey; it's all right, I tell you. Away with you, Johnson—Shannon—for God's sake don't make a crowd of us. I'll talk to you of this in the morning. This is no hour to be debating and whispering here, with the captain and mate on deck and the lamp burning brightly.'

These words Captain Trollope delivered in swift, imperious whispers. He spoke as the leader of a gang would, and, as obedient

members of a gang might, did those whom he
addressed slink away to their cabins. He
was alone with Burn, to whom he said:

'You must shift your berth. You'll have
to sleep with a man.'

'What the blazes has gone wrong?' exclaimed Burn.

'You shrieked out.'

'What made you dab your hand down
then? Who the deuce wouldn't shriek out,
as you call it, when he's struck in his sleep?'

'You fat fool! A baby would not have
been aroused by my touch. But this is what
I want to tell you: you talk in your sleep;
you're a danger to us; your voice can be
heard through the bulkhead of the adjoining
cabin. You must rout out of this, I tell you,
and sleep with a man.'

'Well, that can be arranged, I suppose?'
said Burn, with a sulky yawn. 'What did I
say in my sleep?'

'You spouted some bosh in blank verse;

you had a quarrel with a stage prompter.'
Burn was broadly grinning. 'Consider,' continued Trollope in a whisper of rage, 'what's
to be the result if you should dream of the
job and argue it out with one of your bottle-
bred phantoms?'

'Well, I admit it *is* dangerous,' said Burn.
'Shall I turn out at once? Where am I to
go?'

Trollope put his head out to look at the
cuddy clock; then exclaimed:

'Oh, I suppose you may be trusted for
the rest of the night. Try to keep awake.'

He yawned himself as he spoke, and without another word slipped across the deck to
his own cabin.

That morning at seven o'clock old Benson
was pacing the poop in goloshes and tall hat.
A couple of seamen were swabbing down the
planks, which glanced in the morning sun
with the brightness of diamonds; the sun-
dried brine flashed with each lazy roll of the

barque, and the vessel seemed on fire with the glory that broke from her decks. The mate, unshorn, and grim with three hours of watch, paced the break of the poop athwart-ships. The sails had a shadowing of dew upon them, and they floated off heavily from their yards and sheets as the swing of the swell put some weight of breeze into their hollows. The yards were braced as square as if the ship was in port. The mainsail was hauled up ; all the after fore and aft canvas brailed in and hauled down, but the main-royal shone on high, and there was air enough to keep the cutwater fretting the clear blue ; lines of ripples rolled harp-like aft, with now and again a flake of foam that dissolved as fast as the eye could catch it.

A beautiful cloudless morning, but misty eastwards, with the splendours of the risen sun, so that it was not until the trembling dazzle had drawn well on to the port bow that captain and mate spied the hulk of a dis-

masted vessel lying almost directly ahead.
Distance made a toy of it to the naked sight.
In the glass it showed as a brig or a schooner,
with painted ports, floating with a comfort-
able height of side.   She was ragged with
trailing wreckage.   There was no smoke—no
signs of life.   Clearly an abandoned craft, to
be caulked by old ocean with weeds and shell
into an unsinkable fabric; to strain southward
and dance to the thunders of terrible weather
in the vast hollow seas of the Southern Cross.
Such an object, eternally buoyant with the
caulking irons of Neptune, the whaleman sees
at night by the icy glare of the moon in the
north as he storms before the gale.   It is
sometimes robed in the Leviathan weed of
those wild seas, and flogs the snow-darkened
hurricane with livid kelp as it soars to the
boiling peak.

Neither the captain nor the mate of the
Queen, however, was of a sentimental turn.
They saw no poetry nor any possibilities of

romance in anything their eye rested upon,
even though it were the shooting colours of
the Aurora, or an angry Atlantic sunset.

'A dismasted vessel right ahead, sir,'
says Mr. Matthews, looking round.

'I see it, sir,' says old Benson, and then
he fetched the glass.

Whilst the old skipper was working away
with the telescope, Trollope came up through
the companion hatch.

'Good morning, sir,' says Captain Trollope, 'another fine day, but at this pace the
Queen is not going to keep her promise of a
ten-week run.'

'Perhaps not, sir,' answered old Benson,
with an unconscious sneer and an impatient
glance aloft.

'I am asked by Mr. Burn to apologise to
you, captain, for the row he kicked up in the
night. It was pure nightmare, he believes.'

'It alarmed the ladies,' said the captain
shortly.

'He fears he might repeat it if left alone,' continued Trollope. 'I suppose there is no objection to his changing his berth?'

'None, sir, if he can find another. He can speak to the steward on the subject.' He was about to step forward, when, rounding on his goloshes, he exclaimed, lifting up his face and staring hard into the eyes of Captain Trollope:

'Were you acquainted with Mr. Burn before you met him in this ship?'

'No,' answered Trollope, coolly meeting the old fellow's gaze. 'Why do you ask?'

'I had thought you were friends before , you joined the vessel.'

'No, sir.'

The skipper walked forward to where the mate trudged. Captain Trollope went to the rail, and saw the wreck ahead; he leaned with folded arms, gazing listlessly at it, as at something that bored and sickened him. From time to time he flashed the glance of an eagle from under his drooping lids at the skipper and mate as they stood together. He looked a fine figure of man, soldierly, of proportions heroic when compared with the stump-ended frames of the two battered seamen at the other end of the deck. But that upward curl of nose played the deuce with his beauty.

'There is a something,' said Captain Benson to his mate after looking round to observe if the man was out of hearing, 'in some of the passengers which I do not understand, and, not understanding, do not like. You at the foot of the table hear more of their talk than I. I make ten of them. They seem to have met before.'

'I've gathered that, sir,' answered the mate.

'Captain Trollope yonder denies previous acquaintance with the gentleman who howled last night.'

'He may have a reason for saying it,'

answered Mr. Matthews. 'I will keep my ears open, sir. I believe I shall be able to satisfy myself that he has not told you the truth.'

It was not often that old Benson unbent himself thus to his mate. He was now somewhat restless in mind. Some half-formed suspicion, incredible, incommunicable, teased him.

'They all seem gentlemen, though, Mr. Matthews,' says he, with another look around to see what had become of Captain Trollope.

'They are that, sir,' answered the mate, 'there's breeding in their speech. Some are very respectably connected, I judge, from what's now and again let fall at table.'

'Endeavour to find out, sir,' said the captain, speaking softly, 'if they were known one to another, before they booked their passage.'

'Ay, ay, sir.'

'Ten men, you see, all showing like gentlemen of broken fortunes, desperate with ill-success in the colonies and with having to face life in England penniless—all of them previously acquainted—' here the old chap's broken sentences fined down into a rumble, at which the mate strained his ears in vain. 'But how should I know they're penniless?' continued Benson.

'They have a castaway air, one and all, sir,' said the mate, who was attending to his captain's speech with a face of growing astonishment.

'It is *that*, perhaps,' continued the skipper. 'What luggage did they bring?'

'Nothing that needed stowing under hatches,' answered the mate with a slow smile.

The captain was about to speak. The first stroke of eight bells checked him.

'You have my instructions, sir,' said he, speaking through the chimes.

Mr. Matthews touched his cap, and the captain walked aft where several of the passengers stood viewing the wreck.

CHAPTER V

THE WRECK

THERE was poetic insight in the remark of the lady passenger that a solitary object encountered upon the ocean, whether a ship in full sail, or such an abandoned craft as that out yonder ahead of the *Queen*, changes the face of the deep by imparting a quality of melancholy through mere compulsion of the sight to realise the mighty distances. It was eight bells, and the wreck was about three miles off; the fiery sun was eating into the heart of the wind, and the barque's languid crawling threatened tardy approach to the impatient.

The ship's telescope went the rounds : all were agreed that no signs of life were visible aboard the hulk. The horizon swam in silver past her, and her sheathing flashed in wet dazzling stars as the long cradling Pacific heave slightly rolled her.

'*She* would have given us the chance,' said Mark Davenire to Captain Trollope as they stood together at the mizzen rigging.

'Yes, I see your meaning,' said the other. 'But she comes too soon,' and he rolled his keen eye at the *Queen's* longboat, and then at her quarter boat, as though one thought put another into his head. 'I'll tell you what it is,' he continued, speaking almost in a mumble under his heavy moustache. 'The mob of us must be devilish wary, hold apart, and talk little or nothing at table if we're to run daylight into this errand. Here we are two days out; here am I a first-class passenger; yet by the blood of my heart, as my old colonel would say, that gimblet-eyed skipper was as insolently blunt and suspicious just now as if I had been a stowaway, brought aft to him black with the fore-peak, by one of his Jacks.'

'There are too many of us,' said Davenire.

'Yes; less could have managed.'

'Masters may be all right. But drink hasn't burnt the vanity out of him. If he goes messing about with Miss Mansel, some-thing may be said, some feather-light hint unconsciously dropped—she has eyes like corkscrews, and ears like hatchways.'

'How do you know?'

'She watches us.'

Captain Trollope made no answer. A moment later the breakfast bell rang. The wreck was now within a half-hour's reach as the pace then was; the passengers hurried into the saloon to breakfast quickly that they might see the show as it passed within musket-shot, unless the *Queen's* helm was shifted.

'Are we to meet with any more excite-ments?' exclaimed Mrs. Peacock to the captain.

'What is to be understood by that word, ma'am?' answered old Benson.

'Every item in the catalogue of naval disaster,' said Mr. Storr.

'Any bargains to be had in that catalogue?' called out Mr. Burn, smiling at the little auctioneer whilst he filled a tumbler with a draught of Bass's beer.

'Midnight yells should go cheap,' answered Mr. Storr, with a sarcastic leer at the fat man.

'I wish that fool Burn would shut up,' exclaimed Trollope to his neighbour, and he leaned forward to catch a sight of him.

'There are no excitements to be expected, ma'am,' said the captain.

'I hope we shall meet with plenty,' exclaimed Miss Holroyd, a kindly faced young woman of two-and-twenty, destitute of personal attractions.

'You must consider, my dear,' said Mrs. Peacock, a little severely, 'that I am making this voyage for my health.'

Captain Trollope, wiping his moustache, rose from the table and stalked out on to the quarterdeck. A few followed, then the whole table rose, and by that time the wreck was close aboard on the starboard bow.

She was a plain little hull; had possibly been some New Zealand or Australian keel trading to the islands. Her long tiller swept from bulwark to bulwark, as she rolled, like a human arm wild with appeal. The whiteness of every splintered thing told of recent disaster. In the water under her port haunch was a wonderful brilliant, sparkling, and multitudinous flashing of minute azure and silver lights: the whole rose and fell in splendid gleams with the motions of the hull and the lift of the sea.

'What can that be, captain?' inquired Mrs. Holroyd.

'Fish, ma'am,' responded the skipper, and he put a binocular glass into the lady's hand.

And fish that swelling knoll of brilliance

was, the biggest of the length of your finger, by what courted, and by what detained, who can tell? There was no grass on the sheathing: nothing good for fish to eat; the lovely cloud shone beautiful in the blue water in the shadow of the wreck. Nobody had seen such a sight before, and passengers and seamen lining the rail stared their hardest. Mr. Poole, stepping aft to the captain with a flourish of his thumb to his cap, said in a low voice :

'I fancy there's life aboard that craft, sir. I see a sort of vapour oozing out of the caboose chimney as though the fire was not long out.'

The captain took his glass from Mrs. Holroyd, and suddenly said with emphasis, 'It's as you say, sir. Take and board and overhaul her.'

A boat was lowered, and the second officer and four seamen pulled away for the hull. Even as the boat started, the black wet gleaming curve of a grampus showed between

the wreck and the barque; it breathed in a
sigh that was as music for the silent poetry of
that hull; instantly the shining cloud under
the wreck's quarter sank and vanished.

Three of the set who may now be called
the ten, stood smoking their pipes in the
gangway watching the boat and the hull,
but conversing in low voices. The helm of
the *Queen* had been put down, the lighter
canvas trembled in floating fingers of sunshine and shadow high aloft, the ripple had
died at the cutwater; the cook stepped out
of the galley, hot and cursing, to empty a
bucket of his galley parings over the side,
and the stuff floated motionless.

'I tell you what,' says Mr. Caldwell to
Mr. Masters, standing in the gangway, 'if that
hull there hadn't come too soon she'd have
saved us the most troublesome part of the
job.'

'No, man,' answered Mr. Masters; 'what
could we have to say to a dismasted vessel?

There's to be no cruelty, you know, and a
fortnight of a crowd in that thing there would
make a hell of her.'

Caldwell gazed at him with a black
thoughtful scowl; he was the most savage-
looking of the lot, with a sullen motion of
blood-stained eye when talking, though he
could be nimble enough with his sight when
he chose.

'What ocean d'ye think this is, Masters?'
said Mr. Peter Johnson, who was one of the
three.

'Hanged if I know! The Pacific, I
suppose.'

'And the heart of it, too,' says Mr. Peter
Johnson. 'If this water could be kept
smooth, you'd see the gleams of the wakes of
whalers crossing and recrossing one another.
Nothing but whalers here. How long has
yonder vessel been in that state? Probably
not three days. And here's a splendid little
ship already alongside of her, willing, I pre-

sume, to do anything and everything in the name of humanity. What the deuce, then! Where would the cruelty be? I'd board her and take my chance of a rescue in twenty-four hours for a hundred sovereigns. Well, no, not in twenty-four hours,' says he, with a look up at the lofty serene sky.

'Where have they put Burn?' said Masters.

'Along with Shannon,' answered Caldwell. 'Davenire takes his berth. Shannon will have a bucket of cold water at hand, and it is agreed that he shall tilt a drencher over the squealer should ever he start on one of his midnight sweeteners again.'

Meanwhile, watched with deep interest by all the passengers on the poop, the boat reached the side of the wreck, where she was manœuvred so as to board clear of the trailing raffle. Mr. Poole sprang into the main-chains, and was followed by a seaman. The others shoved off and hung within easy hail.

There was nothing for a sailor's eye to critically consider in this little craft. She had apparently been rigged as a brigantine. Scores of such fabrics you may observe any day in the sea-ports of the old home, lying alongside quays, ballast rattling into their holds, cargo springing to the leaps of coal-blackened men. She was without a boat; portions of the bulwarks had been crushed flat to the waterway. She was as sheer a little hulk as ever made piteous appeal out of nakedness to the careless eye of the passing mariner; tight in her timbers, however, Mr. Poole thought her when his experienced tread felt into each heave and found it buoyant.

She had a small deck cabin aft with two windows, and a door looking forward; and forward, just abaft the galley, was a house in which her seamen had slung their hammocks. Poole and the sailor went first of all to look at the galley fire. They stared about them as they went. Her decks were comparatively clear, and it was certain she had been a light ship, bound for a cargo.

What man on boarding derelicts of this sort can conjecture the sight that is to greet him? Death at sea is a horribly fanciful artist. Poole remembered once boarding a vessel abandoned as this was, and being confronted on getting over the side by a frightful mask of face that swayed and moved in the cage of a heap of fallen shrouds. He was for flying; the mask had a firm squint, and was moustachioed. Its gestures conveyed a ghastly threat to Poole; but rallying his heart and looking close, the mate beheld the figure of a dead man so entangled in the rigging, whose ends lay over the side, that at every lift of swell the head motioned a living menace.

There was nothing of the kind, however, to be seen here. Poole and the man walked warily to the galley and peered into a tiny caboose with a tiled floor, a sort of sentry box seized to the deck. Strange it had not gone with the masts. Some brown coal vapour, thin as the smoke from a tobacco-pipe, lazily crawled into the chimney out of the almost extinct embers of a fire. So then she had not been long abandoned.

They looked into the deck-house and found nothing but a few hammocks and some odds and ends of clothes. Mr. Poole hailed the *Queen.*

'Hallo!' sang back old Captain Benson.

'Maybe, sir, if you were to send a hand aloft with the glass he'll make out signs of a boat, for the galley-fire's not yet out.'

The white-haired skipper raised his hand, and Mr. Poole followed by the sailor went aft.

They had gained the gangway, and were within a dozen paces of the door of the after deck-house, when they came to a halt as though shot or paralysed. Full in the door-way stood a figure. It was a man of about thirty, naked to the waist. His breeches were of floating dungaree, and his feet were naked. The sad sight to behold—the bad, most afflicting part to see, was his face. He was grinning with the withered smile of consumption. The puckering about the mouth was like a hunchback's. His teeth lay naked to the full width of the distended lips, and they made the whole face as un-meaning and mocking as a skull. His hair was brown, soft and long, his eyes too were brown and might not have been wanting in beauty; but the brilliance of famine or mad-ness was in them now.

'Father of light, what's this?' cried Mr. Poole.

The poor creature put his finger to his lips; his smile vanished. He made a beckon-ing gesture with a short sailorly bow as of entreaty. Poole went up to him.

'Are there more of you?' said he.

'Stop!' cried the man with a peculiar hard accent that might have been a Welshman's,

'I have been waiting for this chance. Come with me, sir,' and the half-naked figure turned and led the way into the cabin. Mr. Poole looked quickly about him expecting to see others, or fearing to find the dying or the dead, or, which would have been worse, more lunatics. It was a narrow interior, snug enough, cabined on one hand with one central table and a line of lockers for seats. Upon the table lay a chart which the half-naked man went straight up to. He passed his fingers through his hair, and looking round at Mr. Poole who now fearlessly stood close, he put his forefinger upon the chart and exclaimed in his harsh almost hissing accents:

'Is this or is this not the situation of this vessel?'

Mr. Poole bent his head and perceived that it was a chart of the North Sea.

'Never mind about the ship's place,' said he soothingly. 'Are there more of you? My vessel waits for us.'

'Why don't you answer me?' exclaimed the madman, stooping his face close to the spot his finger still rested upon. 'All yesterday I was trying to find it out. The latitude and longitude's wrong. Can't I fix a ship's situation on a chart as well as another? I'll pit my whole stock of blood against any man's as a navigator. No sun to take, for it was dark all last night. And when there is a sun he spins like a Tyneside grindstone round the horizon. Oh, it makes me sweat,' he cried, fetching his naked chest a slap that made Mr. Poole skip a pace or two clear of him.

'Let me deal with him, sir,' said the sailor, whispering hoarsely into the second mate's ear. 'I've got a brother-in-law that's locked up. Ye must match artfulness with artfulness along with the likes of this.'

'Shove ahead then,' said Mr. Poole.

'Beg pardon, I'm sure,' said the seaman, stepping to the madman's side. 'But let me see;' here he thrust his nose at the chart, it was a hundred to one if he could read. 'Why, of course! this to be sure must be the vessel's sittivation.' The madman listened with a face of teeth and hair that might have expressed satisfaction or conviction had he been sane. 'But I must tell yer,' continued the sailor, 'there's an old gentleman called Captain Benson, close aboard, who'll be happy, I'm sure, to compare his charts with yourn. Suppose you come and have a talk with him.'

The poor creature's brown eyes glared suspiciously. He looked up through the little skylight, round the cabin, then at his naked trunk which he on a sudden hugged with a maiden's modesty.

'Where shall I find your clothes?' said the second mate.

The madman took no notice. He pointed again at the chart, and looking at the seaman said:

'Does the old gentleman know anything about navigation?'

'Know? Why, he can tell where he is by the sun arter she's set. A lonesome star of a thick night will put him within a hinch of his true place. The Hadmirality have offered him pounds a week to navigate their fleets, but he don't like the notion of wearin' a uniform.'

The wretch gave a crazy nod which made his smile terrific. Mr. Poole pulled off his coat and buttoned it over the shoulders of the madman. Whilst this was doing he said to the seaman: 'Look into these cabins, whilst I get this man to the boat. Come along, sir,' said he, blandly, ' and I will introduce you to the old gentleman.'

'Without my chart?' shrieked the madman.

The second mate rolled the North Sea up and fixed it as a telescope under the poor fellow's arm.

The *Queen* lay close in with the wreck, and what passed aboard was quite easily

visible to the naked eyes of the passengers.
There had been life then in that derelict, and
one poor miserable human sufferer was to be
delivered from a horrible death! Yonder
dismasted fabric, swaying in the flash of the
brine, with now a lift of green sheathing, and
now a dip of her painted ports, takes the
tragic and thrilling significance of human
suffering itself from the spectacle of one man
as he is landed into the boat, flourishing his
naked arms, and talking and halloing to the
ship.

'Did not you promise that we should
meet with no more horrors, captain?' said
Mrs. Peacock to old Benson.

The commander wiped his weather-dis-
coloured face with a red pocket handkerchief
big as a small ensign, and answered, 'There
can be no horror in the saving of a man's life,
ma'am.'

'He is mad!' exclaimed Mrs. Peacock,
watching the man as he approached the boat.

'I cannot help it,' answered Captain Benson.

'Good Giddens!' murmured Johnson to Burn, catching the special point of the incident with discernment worthy of a loftier mind. 'It would just be that pendulum-swaying that would craze me. See how wearily and regularly she rolls, but without way. It would work the wits loose in the brain: they would pitch from side to side like shifting ballast, and the continual hammering of them upon the skull, first on this side, then on that, would set me grinning and raving just like yonder coon in a very few hours.'

'He would be nearly naked,' said Mr. Burn in his oozy voice, ' but for the mate's coat. Why should a man when he goes daft always want to strip himself? Is it because madness brings a chap close to his original state of nature?'

'Here he comes,' said Mr. Johnson ; ' stand by for a rush of ladies.'

'Where's the captain?' shouted the madman as he bounded over the rail, delivering
himself eel-like from the grip of a seaman,
and dropping the second mate's coat overboard in the swift struggle. He had kept a
hold of his chart, however, and now flourished
it as he screamed : ' Where's the captain ? '

'Lay aft some hands and secure that poor
fellow,' shouted old Benson, travelling forwards
to the break of the poop with incredible
activity.

Before this command could be attended
to the lunatic was at his side.

'This is the chart, sir,' he cried, unrolling
it with insane vehemence, whilst the ladies
in a body rushed below, leaving Mr. Dent and
Mr. Storr standing at the companion way
ready for immediate flight. ' They tell me
you're a first-class navigator. I can't make
the ship's situation right. Look here ! '

Old Benson saw that the chart represented
the North Sea.

'The sun,' cried the lunatic as he stared for a breath with an eagle's unwinking eye at the blazing luminary, ' goes round and round like a horse in a circus. Can *you* catch him?' he asked in a hissing whisper, with a horrible grin of cunning. ' He don't shine of a night, and all day long he gallops round and round.'

By this time, however, the surgeon, the second mate, and some seamen had gathered about the poor creature. He yelled when they were obliged to use force. His shrieks on the quarter-deck rang in echoes from the silent hollows of the sails, and you seemed to hear a faint answer to them trembling in a sort of moan aboard the wreck. He had the sense to see he was not to be returned to his vessel, and his craving was for *her*. It took half the ship's company to get him forward. They stowed him away in a wing cabin, securely bound, and a sailor watched him.

How long was this voyage going to

occupy, some of the passengers wondered. It seemed but a few hours ago that they had sailed out of Sydney Harbour, yet in that time so much had happened, a whole round voyage of prosaic steam might contain less incident. But that's the way of the sea. The noise of whales blowing their fountains in the dark; the loveliness of a level plain of ocean scored by ice-like swathes, the horizon melting into a delicate faintness of hot blue, with one white sail reeling and winding in the air afar; or the staggering ship with the rigging full of figures, and an ensign of appeal shrieking in rags at its seizings, the whole plunging fabric pale with the sheeting of spray through whose flashful drifts you behold the curved and freckled backs of huge green seas, scourged into spitting and frothing madness by the cold and steady gale, rushing into the dimness of the horizon, but how to catalogue the sights and revelations of the deep?

These and a thousand like create the life of tacks and sheets, all the romance of the fabric of sail from truck to waterline; they serve as plates to embellish the plain tale of a voyage. The story of the inner life of the ship goes on as the vessel sails along, and these strange details of wrecks and madmen, of open boats and throat-sucking thirst, of the gleam of the grampus and the subsidence of a knoll of gem-like fish, drift leisurely by and vanish far astern.

The *Queen* was brought to her course, her sails slept to the light air, and their silver trembled under the shadow of her hull. The wreck slided away, forlornly rocking.

'You are certain there was nobody else on board, sir?' said Captain Benson to the second mate.

'Certain, sir.'

'Who is this madman?'

'The mate, I allow, sir—he hasn't the

looks of the captain—gone loose-headed on a sudden with loneliness.'

'Or grief,' said Captain Benson, casting his eyes upon Mr. Storr, who stood listening. 'There may have been a wife or some one dear to the man lost to him in that business,' said he with a nod at the wreck.

The second mate smiled with surprise at this effort of sentiment on the part of the skipper. Sentiment is not esteemed at sea. They say that no man who is sentimental can make a sailor; no man who can admire a glorious sunset or watch fascinated from the flying jibboom end the spectacle of his full-rigged ship shearing at him with froth-clouded bows through the water, can make a sailor! God help ye, Jack, then, if this be so. But after all this may be but the opinion of brutal theorists.

'Is there any chance for the man?' said the captain, addressing the surgeon as he came up the poop ladder.

The surgeon shook his head. 'He howls like a wolf,' said he; 'he might have lived another week in that wreck yonder, but the sun won't rise upon him alive to-morrow in this ship.'

'Lor!' said Captain Benson.

It befel as the surgeon predicted; a little time before the first dinner-bell rang, and when the poop was alive with the passengers moving leisurely in the violet twilight of the awning, a seaman came hurriedly out of the berth in which the madman lay confined, and just when the dinner-bell was ringing, and the passengers were going below to prepare themselves for the table, the doctor came aft to the skipper, who stood grasping the brass rail at the break of the poop in a posture of expectation, and exclaimed 'He is dead.'

'Then, sir, we'll get him stitched up at once and bury him in the morning,' said the captain.

Whilst the passengers were eating, a

couple of seamen stood over the dead body forward, stitching it up in a piece of sailcloth ready for the last toss. One of the two was the man who had been set to watch the lunatic. He drove his needle with a pale hard face.

'Bill,' said he presently, when they had stitched the face out of sight, 'do the likes of these here have immortal souls?'

Bill was a man of some colour in his blood; he turned his eyes, dusky and almost as bland as an African's, upon his mate.

'I guess if he was a sailor,' he answered, 'no soul was ever sarved out to him, mad or not mad.'

'Ain't sailors allowed souls, then?'

'Ask it of yourself, Tom,'· answered Bill, in a voice of mingled indifference and contempt.

Tom stopped in his work. The polished needle he held gleamed like fire in a flash of westering sun striking through the little scuttle; he looked at his mate with a face awork with agitation; an emotional man one could easily see he was, a sailor of the snuffling sort, yet smart and skilful.

'Am I to believe,' says he, laying one hand not without reverence on the dead body, 'that this pore chap didn't have no soul to go to God with?'

'Ye can believe what yer like,' answered the other, 'but I'll tell you what it is; the more you believe the more yer'll be warping yer intellects to the bearings this covey's was brought to. Let's bear a hand with the job. 'Taint all jam.'

They stitched in silence, and when they had made a bolster-shaped parcel of the body they carried it out in obedience to instructions, and placed it upon the fore hatch, and Tom went aft for an ensign to cover it with.

It was the second dog watch, a lovely evening, the ship in full sail, the low sun lighting up all the west in red glory. The cook lounged out of the galley with a cigar in his mouth, and his hat rakishly tilted toward his left eye; he looked at the body, and asked Tom, who was in the act of throwing the ensign over it, when it was to be chucked overboard. The seaman answered with a solemn silent shake of the head.

'Why must they go and bring them things for'rads?' continued the cook, albeit with a careful glance aft to make sure of his audience. 'Everything that's disgusting,' said he with a voice of affectation, 'comes for'rads. Is it a dead body? Is it uneatable meat? Is it spuds like tumours and flour that laughs in your face with the maggots that tumbles the surface of it—it must all come for'rads.'

Some seamen approached and lounged at the bulwarks abreast to listen.

'Ain't it enough that men should have to sign for a working day of twenty-four hours,' continued the cook, breaking up his speech with occasional puffs at his cigar, 'that everything bad should come for'rads? There's a body,' says he pointing. 'He was a mate, they say; why don't they keep him aft? Mates bunk and mess aft when they're alive; why shouldn't they bunk if they can't mess aft arter they're dead? No. They must be brought for'rads. When they're carrion they become proper for common sailors to consort with.'

'Bloomed if it ain't every word true though,' said one of the loungers at the rail.

'Is there e'er a man here that can answer me this question?' exclaimed Tom, who, having covered the body, was leaning against the foremast with a knife and a plug of tobacco in his hands; 'had ever that chap a soul?'

'I allow that if *you* have *he* had,' said the cook, with a look at the little row of loafers.

'It's hard, it's hard,' cried Tom, flourish-

ing his knife and plug of tobacco, ' that a
man should be denied a soul because he goes
mad. I say, whoever says it, lies! I liken
madness to a storm o' wind. The waves beat
and the ship jumps, but the soul,' he said,
with a pale smile, ' sits snug within, quite
sane, a-knowing all about it, incapable of
action 'cos of the dishorganisation outside,
but fit and in proper trim to go aloft when
the time comes,' he added, with a look at the
body, ' where it'll receive more pity, and in
my opinion stand a better chance, than some
who enjoys the use of their senses down to
the hour of their being brought-to.' Saying
which, with a rather wild face, he made for
the forecastle entrance, and disappeared, talking to himself.

' Fired if I don't think Tom's been turned
daft by watching of it,' said one of the
loungers, indicating the body with a lift of
his chin.

' Tom's one as sails about with an anchor

over his bows, ready to let go, but can't find soundin's to bring up in,' said another of the loungers.

A sudden call from the poop broke up this conversation.

At eight bells the cook locked up his galley, and the first watch began. Another fine night of waters, rippling in moonshine! The barque, with starboard overhanging studding sails, floated like ice through the moon-whitened air, and many trembling stars studded the arches between the sails; and under the yawn of the fore course the lamps of heaven shone like distant lighthouses. A seaman walked the deck of the little fore-castle on the look-out. The rest of the watch had stowed themselves away for a nap abaft the longboat, and in the deep shadows under the bulwarks; they gave the dead body as wide a berth as they could, and the watch below turned in growling that the thing should be so near them.

The least of Jack's loves is a dead man
as a shipmate.

The ship had tripped, so to speak, over
four dead bodies already since the start, and
a hairy man, his legs thrown over his hammock edge, disclosing toes with nails which
looked like shoe-horns, asked in a gruff voice,
after sucking out the last spark in his pipe,
if 'these here deaths didn't mean death to
the blushen ship too in the end.' This
started some superstitious jawing among the
fools, and hammock answered hammock, till
a passionate voice in the dusk of 'the eyes'
bawled for silence and sleep.

Two men came down from the poop
smoking pipes, and going along to the fore-
hatch, stopped and looked at the body.

'That's much how it would have been
with me,' said Mr. Mark Davenire; 'a toss
and a bubble, and not the memory of a
moment, by Jove, to follow me!'

'Better that than death in the bush,' said

Mr. Hankey, 'where, if the fowls of the air permit, you rot into a grin of bones. There's a beastly baseness in the disclosure of one's marrow-pipes. I should wish to lie secret, or at least hidden, as that chap will be when he's over the side. I'd not even that the moon should shine upon my skeleton,' and the man's face looked up pale, betwixt its hard black whiskers, at the planet that was softly glowing over the port beam. They began to pace the deck to and fro abreast of the corpse.

'When is our business to be done?' said Hankey in a quiet voice. 'Trollope seems to hang in the wind. Is not this the right sort of weather? Why not make an end of it this very night? Are we waiting for the Horn?'

Davenire hissed a cautious 'hush' as a sailor stumbled up out of the shadow of the longboat, and passed them to mount the forecastle ladder, where he joined the fellow on the look-out.

'The ship must reach the agreed situation,' said Davenire, speaking with a note of authority, as a leader or lieutenant. 'Trollope isn't sure; besides that, old Benson's on the watch. Bosh! the old cock stares, and I find him brusque as Trollope does, as though distrustful. But what in the name of holy Jimmy *can* he suspect? Any way, if the job's to be done, it must be rushed effectually. There's to be no opposition, *and no bloodshed*. That must be seen to. It's not to be a hanging affair.'

'When is that arms-chest to be dealt with?' said Hankey.

'Presently. I should have thought you'd see that,' said Davenire, dryly.

Hankey wagged his head in the moonshine.

'Hark!' exclaimed Davenire, 'what are those two chaps up there arguing about?'

The look-out man and the seaman who had joined him came to a stand at the head of the forecastle ladder. They did not appear to heed the presence of the two gentlemen, who, moving a few paces forward, halted to listen in the shadow of the berth in which the body had lain. From the poop lightly floated the voices of passengers in conversation, mingled with the music of a piano in the cuddy, faint with the intervention of mizzenmast and cuddy front, and you could hear the high tones of a woman singing.

'Don't you make no mistake,' said the voice of the seaman named Tom, 'you've never tarned to and thought over things as I have, Bill.'

'Why, no,' answered Bill; 'and I've kept my senses in consequence.'

'Ha!' exclaimed Tom, panting out the word with the noise of a heavy snore, 'it's fearful to think if a chap's head's agoing wrong his soul's bound to go wrong too. What's the soul? Can ye explain it? Is it

part of the physical faculties, or a separate
hessence which breaks away from the dead
body just as the smoke of a candle goes up
arter the flame's blowed out? Lor' bless me,
what's a happening to my head? Fired if
my brains ain't been jammed by the girth of
this here cap,' and the listeners heard the
man fling his cap violently on to the deck.

The other walked silently into the bows
of the ship.

'That fellow's losing the right time in his
works, isn't he?' said Hankey, as the two
strolled leisurely aft, turning for a moment to
look at the figure of the man who was standing motionless in the moonlight like a shape
of ebony, with his eyes seemingly fixed upon
his cap at his feet.

'There's always a religious seaman in a
long-voyage forecastle,' said Davenire.

'He's needed,' said his companion.

'I remember a man,' continued Davenire,
'who, before the voyage was ended, got two-

thirds of what had been the profanest set of blasphemers that ever slept in a forecastle, to regularly assemble at a prayer meeting in the first dog-watch. He was a pale man, with large spiritual eyeballs. He got first one and then two to listen to him. It was slow work, but he persevered. The passengers made him a purse before the ship's arrival, and he distributed the money amongst his congregation, refusing to take a penny piece. That was——'

He was interrupted by a loud groan or cry of ' Jesus, receive me!' immediately followed by the splash of a body.

' Man overboard !' yelled a voice from the forecastle head.

' Hanged if it isn't that pious seaman!' cried Davenire, and he and his friend rushed on to the poop.

' Help! help!' shouted a voice alongside. ' Pick me up, afore I'm drownded. Good Lord, what have I gone and done!'

The fine white moonlight was so clear you could distinctly see the man's upturned face as he struck out. The ship slowly drove past. Some of the ladies were screaming. Mr. Poole, who had the watch, sprang to the quarter, and with both hands launched a large life-buoy quoit-like. It struck the swimmer, who was shouting for help, and he went under, but was up again in a minute, and floated, holding on to the life-buoy, bubbling and bawling, whilst the ship was gradually coming round to the wind.

They got him aboard, after some bothering with the boat. Old Benson, in his tall hat, stood stern and firm at the head of the poop ladder; the shadows of his legs, painted by the moon on the white plank, might have framed some gigantic egg with its top sliced off. All the passengers had gathered near him to view the drenched man lifted over the rail; some of the ladies trembled and fanned themselves, and Mr. Dent looked scared and white in the pale light. The half-drowned man stood upright, hatless, with plastered hair, and a gleaming wet shadow spread at his feet.

'Is he able to speak?' cried the captain.

'Are you able to speak?' shouted Mr. Poole in the man's ear.

'Why, yes,' answered the fellow, passing his sopping arm over his streaming face. 'What's it all about? Gi' us a drop of liquor, some 'un.'

'Did he fall overboard?' demanded the captain.

'He threw himself overboard, sir,' sang out a voice from the boat's falls.

'Gi' us a drop. My senses are all abroad,' said the man.

Captain Trollope went down the port poop ladder. He pulled a flask of brandy from his pocket, and the soaked and crazy seaman drained a couple of gills. Then his teeth began to chatter, and he trembled violently.

'Did you fall overboard?' shouted old Benson.

'I chucked myself overboard,' answered the fellow, in a shuddering, whispering voice.

'Chucked yourself overboard!' cried the literal captain. 'D'ye mean to tell me you meant to drown yourself aboard my ship?'

'Not arter I was in the water,' replied the man, looking at Captain Trollope as though for another sup.

'Take him forward—take him forward!' shouted the skipper, in accents of horror and rage.

'I thought I was going mad,' cried the man, 'and that I could only save my soul by perishing first.'

'Take him forward,' bawled the captain; 'and, Mr. Poole, set a watch over him.'

'I'm calm now. I feel it's all right. The wetting's done me sights of good. It's all along of watching that chap on the hatch,' exclaimed the man.

But here Mr. Poole and others fell to shoving him, and in a few moments the hustling group walked forward, and vanished like smoke in the dusk of the forecastle.

CHAPTER VI

THE ARMS-CHEST

WHEN Captain Benson came on deck early
next morning the sailors were washing down,
and the ship was stretching along under full
breasts of canvas; a smart breeze had come
on to blow in the middle watch; the ocean
was pouring steadily out of the south-west;
past the foam of the ridge abeam, as the
Queen rose, you could make out three white
spires—a big ship, bound like the barque, no
doubt, round the Horn. The seething blue
hollows astern were freckled with small white
sea-fowl. They had no business so far north;
you meet them gleaming over waters whose
skies are whitened by giant fields of ice.
They raced after the *Queen*, faultlessly mould-

ing their flight to the heave of the sea, and they filled with interest, beautiful and living, the wide yeast of the wake that rushed off astern, whiter and more defined than a London coaching road.

The captain looked at those birds for a few minutes and then round upon the sea, letting his gaze rest upon the three shining needles abeam. He now called the mate to him.

'How is that man who threw himself overboard last night?'

'All right, sir;' and the mate pointed to the fellow, who was scrubbing, with an earnest face, at the deck near the main-mast.

'Is he safe to be at large?'

'I've overhauled him and believe he is, sir. The man's a fair sailor and sound enough; but he's of a pious cast, and his brain got shifted by watching the lunatic yesterday.'

'We'll bury the body at five bells,' said the captain.

' Ay, ay, sir.'

The captain looked hard at the sailor, as though he reasoned within himself whether he should call him aft and rate him; then, perhaps guessing that the mate had done all that was necessary in that way, he was rounding on the flat soles of his goloshes, when he stopped again and said, with a glance along the poop :

'Have you found anything worth making a note of at your end of the table, sir?'

'Why, no, sir; since you spoke to me on the subject I have found the people very cautious in their conversation.'

'Is it to be ascertained who Captain Trollope is?' said the captain.

'Some of the gentlemen may know, but will they give us the truth? There's Mr. Dent, sir; or some of the ladies, perhaps——'

'They have inquired of me,' interrupted

the captain, hastily. 'I don't like his looks, sir.'

'And yet, but for his nose, a tall, fine, gentlemanly man, sir.'

'I don't like his looks, sir,' repeated the captain, hotly; 'and I don't like the looks of the man they call Masters. Whilst, as to Mr. Caldwell'—here he peered cautiously round—'I wouldn't have a man with *his* face in my forecastle.'

Mr. Matthews let sink his head in thought. He was puzzled by the captain's suspicions, yet not more, perhaps, than the old fellow himself was by them. What were they to fear? A mutiny of ten passengers? There could be no mutiny where there was no authority, and the ten gentlemen, moreover, seemed perfectly happy. They had praised the ship's Marsala, they ate heartily of the galley's various dishes, they lounged in groups and talked together quietly, smoking on the quarter-deck, or conversing with the ladies in a very gentlemanly way indeed. Why was the captain suspicious, then? thought the mate, as he walked with a grave and sober face to the athwartship rail to watch the fellows washing down the quarter-deck.

A small gloom overhung the spirits of the breakfast-table that morning. A dead man was in the ship, and he was to be buried.

'When is the funeral?' asked Mr. Masters of the captain.

'At half-past ten, sir,' answered old Benson, looking sideways at the worn, dissipated, yet still handsome features of the man.

'Were you ever present at a funeral at sea, Miss Mansel?' said Mr. Masters.

'Never,' answered the girl, with a slight, unconscious shudder.

'There's a poem on the subject. I used to know it when I was a lad,' said Mr. Storr.

'A hundred thousand poems on the subject,' snarled Mr. Caldwell, turning his dark, gloomy face upon the auctioneer. 'There's nothing in nature that hasn't a poem hitched to it, and some of the best things are tailed like kites, every rhymester knotting on his piece of paper, till the whole dead-weighted show is brought with a sickening thud to earth.'

'You're not fond of poetry, perhaps?' said Mr. Storr doubtfully.

'About as fond of it as Captain Benson is,' answered Mr. Caldwell.

Miss Holroyd tittered, old Benson coloured up. His dignity was mighty impatient of any personal references of that sort. He had made his way aft from the forecastle, and was alarmed by the slightest tone or hint of sarcasm. His only answer was a glance of suspicion down the line of doubtful men on either hand. Captain Trollope looked annoyed, and the conversation sank till the long intervals of silence embarrassed the person who broke it.

At half-past ten they despatched the dead body over the side. Nobody knew whose child he was. No man to have saved his own heart from breaking could have given him his right name. The ladies were affected by the ceremony, and Mrs. Peacock dropped a tear.

The hole the body made in the water did not more swiftly fill than did the memory of the madman fade when old Benson closed his book and passed into the cuddy for his sextant.

This thing is mentioned here, because the log-book of the *Queen* gives it. But for three days after this entry nothing in any way memorable was recorded by the mate. The voyage now looked as though it was to wear a settled face; the seamen gave no trouble; of a dog-watch Tom's deep voice might be heard in argument with the cook or the man Bill by anyone who chose to lounge near the galley, otherwise the fiddle squeaking on the booms perplexed all voices to even the most attentive ear stationed further aft than the long-boat; moreover, the general eye of the poop was engaged and diverted by watching the sailors dancing.

It was the afternoon of the third day that the sparkling fiery blue breeze which had driven the ship forging through it till the lift of the soft cloud of foam on either bow was often as high as the catheads; it was on the afternoon that this sweet-sailing wind failed; it dropped on a sudden like the tail of a blast out of an electric storm; the lofty sails came into the masts with an eager report, as though the ship herself snatched a voice out of this shock of surprise. The run of the seas fell into a smooth swell, which rolled foamless like liquid glass against the dark green of the ship, so exposing her sheathing that on look-ing over the side you saw the reflection blushing like some wavering dart of sunset on the pure round of the water. About two miles on the port beam lay a whaler; the *Queen* had learnt, with the help of flags and a huge blackboard roughly written on with chalk, that she was an American, almost full up, almost three years out, now bound round the Horn for the distant port she would probably take six months in fetching.

A clumsier old waggon never dipped her gangways in a swell, and every lift of her square stern hid from the sight of the people who were looking at her on board the *Queen* the mowing and shining heights of a tall ship hull down. The mercury in the captain's barometer had been steadily sinking since noon. The sky slowly thickened all round, and no sound came from the sea. The swell rolled in breathless heaps, and the white birds vanished. It was the most uncomfortable time the passengers had passed. The ladies could not stand, and the gentlemen staggered, though old Benson observed that most of the men strode the reeling deck with very easy legs—legs of the sea, pliant, elastic, swift in recovery, and a walk that is pleasanter to see than a dance.

Nobody could have supposed that the *Queen* would roll so abominably. She sank to her covering boards, and a nervous ear might easily have found a direct threat of storm in the cannonading of canvas aloft, in the crackling of strained rigging, in noises of breaking crockery, heavy goods fetching away, little shrieks of women, loud calls from the poop, and answering curses from the forecastle. They clewed up and furled down to the topsails, in which they tied two reefs. At one time when this was doing, Trollope and two or three others stood near the mizzen-mast looking up at the main; they swayed easily on their legs like a boy straddling the middle of a swaying see-saw; the reef tackles were then being hauled out, the yard was on the cap, and a few hands were slapping their way up the weather rigging.

'Shall we lend them a hand?' said Mr. Burn, turning to observe the captain, who walked on the quarter.

'I'm game for one,' said Mr. Johnson.

'Quiet!' said Trollope. 'Don't stare aloft. You never seem to know when you're watched.'

'I'm getting blistered sick of waiting,' said Shannon.

'Thunder, how that whaler rolls!' cried Burn.

She was still a clean-cut figure out abeam, but the sail past her had disappeared in the dimness. The spouters were taking a hint from the *Queen* and shortening canvas; with the unaided vision you saw a row of tiny figures dotting the fore-yard, whose points of studding sail boom seemed to spear the very heads of the swell.

'Wash, wash, wash, wash,' muttered Shannon, counting off the monotonous regular steep rolls of the whaler in a sort of ticking way. 'Ancient and fishy will be the smell of blubber that she belches from her hatchways at every plunge. I served six months in one of them . . .'

'We're going to have a black gale,' interrupted Trollope, and he went below.

It was hard to guess by the sinking of the glass what was to happen, saving that a wild, uncomfortable change of some sort was at hand; the workings of the sky were strange and subtle; it was a dirty blue, then it turned of an ashen pallor, a sort of grime thickened upon it till it spread a whole loathsome face of uniform sullen dark green from line to line, with the whaler wallowing dim as a phantom in the hollows, touching the stormy dusk with sudden flashes of white canvas; yet you saw no break of cloud, and the swell, now beginning to lose its weight, ran like grease.

They dined in the cuddy by lamplight. The captain's seat was empty. Mr. Matthews

entered hurriedly for a mouthful and returned, scarcely finding time for the questions
which were discharged at him from the
skipper's end. Mr. Poole was also on deck,
and some one said all hands were on the alert.

Captain Trollope and Mr. Hankey were
the first to quit their seats; they went on the
quarter-deck and stood in the gloom under
the overhanging ledge of the poop. A few
sharp glances followed them, and a knowing
look of arched eyebrow and compressed lip
was darted by Johnson to Cavendish.

On a sudden the captain was heard roaring down the steps for his oilskins, and one of
the stewards ran on deck with a long water-
proof coat.

Hark! What was that?

A sound of the muttering of artillery
behind the sea; next minute the heavens
opened in a violet blaze; a woman screamed
it was as though a mass of fire had fallen
through the skylight into the cuddy; a loud,

but still distant roar followed, and then fell the rain in a living sheet. It shrieked upon the planks overhead, it swelled in the scuppers and floated the loose rigging; it poured like streams from fire-hoses overboard, and still not a breath of air.

Several men left the table and joined Trollope under the poop. The recess here provided as good a shelter as a cabin. There was in the atmosphere an ashen suffusion that yet was not light; you seemed to see, and yet saw not by it; it lay pale on the face like the light of the next world; it was more terrifying than pitch blackness. The gentlemen under the poop sucked their pipes and watched the rain roaring in smoke off the planks. The lightning was now fast and flaming, sheeting over the heavens in twenty confluent forks at a time, and the thunder seemed to split in crashes right over the mast-head. Still no wind.

'I know these storms,' said Davenire;

'there's no gale here. It's going to pass away like a woman in a swoon after a yelling fit.'

'This should give us the opportunity we want,' said Masters.

'We're not ready, and you know it,' exclaimed Captain Trollope. 'Am I to have the handling of this job? I want no suggestions, and much more caution from some of you.'

'What did he say?' exclaimed Burn to Shannon when the thunder had passed.

But before an answer could be made to this question the sea was lighted up by a marvellous, beautiful, but terrific stroke of lightning that fell like a ball some distance away on the port beam of the *Queen*. It flashed through the air as though discharged by some vast gun pointed downwards; a dead unreverberant shock of thunder followed. Some one shouted on the ship's forecastle; there was another cry on the poop overhead.

'What has happened?' cried Mr. Storr,

rushing through the cuddy to the entrance where the men stood.

'The whaler has been struck and is on fire,' answered Captain Trollope, coolly.

He must have had a keen sight and a practised eye to know it, for the lightning made a most dissembling phantom of the Yankee. But he was soon proved right by a light beginning to burn steadily on the sea. The lightning flashed about it, the thunder roared over it; the rain had ceased. A candle flame would have burnt straight in the air. The invisible black swell ran softly, beaten into a low pulse by that great fall of wet, and still yonder light burnt on, growing in brilliancy, till you could see the whaler coming and going to sudden tongues of flame leaping and dying about the foremast.

'Full up with oil. By Jove! what a bonfire we're going to have!' said Mr. Burn.

'A ship on fire!' yelled Mr. Storr into the cuddy.

'Dare we show ourselves?' cried Mrs. Dent, jumping up from the table.

'It don't rain,' answered Mr. Storr; 'the lightning's passing.'

Here Mr. Matthews, sparkling in wet oil-skins, came below to inform the ladies with the captain's compliments that there was a ship on fire in sight, and that if they would care to witness the dreadful spectacle a platform of gratings and dry planking should be at once contrived for them to stand on.

'I would not lose such a sight for a million,' exclaimed Mrs. Dent.

'This sort of thing is called going home for one's health,' said Mrs. Peacock, who had been almost dead with fear during the raging of the storm.

Miss Mansel laughed. However, all of them, including Mrs. Peacock, speedily clothed themselves for the deck, and then the *Queen* was alive with sightseers. The storm was settling northwards, leaving a breathless calm

in its wake ; southwards the evening was
beginning to show in pale stars amidst rifts of
heavy vapour slowly going to pieces.   It
could be seen with the night glass that the
whalemen were fighting the fire, which had
caught a strong hold ; already the bows of the
craft were in flames, and whilst you watched
you could see how those fiery dartings,
snaking into thick smoke, crimsoning it, then
blackening out, coiled their way aft like ser-
pents, with an appearance of frequent repul-
sion, though at every fresh spout of flame
something caught fire a-low and aloft.

'Keep a bright look-out for her boats,'
cried Captain Benson, who walked alone near
the binnacle in short excursions.

He was agitated.   Few sights at sea move
sailors more to their depths than a ship on
fire.   He finds nothing thrilling, splendid, or
romantic in it, as some of the ladies on the
Queen's poop did, as Mr. Storr did now that
the danger of the storm was passed.   To the

sailor a burning ship is the most heartbreak-
ing voice the sea can find a tongue for. You
saw the influence of the sight upon the gang
of men under the break of the poop: they
stood staring, sucking their pipes, dropping
now and then a remark in a sullen note of
helpless sympathy.

'She'll have plenty of boats, though,' said
Mr. Masters.

'Ay; but that don't take the desolation
out of the picture, my friend,' answered Mr.
Burn.

'Fire a rocket, Mr. Matthews, fire a
rocket,' called the captain, his words passing
clear though hoarse through the still air,
' and burn a port-fire,' and he repeated, ' keep
a bright look-out for the boats.'

He slopped his way hastily to the companion, and disappeared, but returned in a
minute, having observed such a rise in the
glass as was good for his spirits.

'Make sail on the ship, sir,' he cried. 'Out

reefs. Loose topgallant sails. Aft here, and set this spanker.'

Whizz went a rocket as he spoke betwixt the two tall masts of the fore and main; a minute later the figure of the second mate overhanging the port was brilliantly outlined against the weltering blackness over the side by a stream of hissing blue fire, fountaining from his hand. There is no effect wilder, more grotesque, more dramatic, more tragic in ghastly suggestion than that produced by the blue light at sea. It lights up a small area of ocean with a hellish complexion, and beyond it all is thunder-blackness. It makes spectres and demons of the shapes of men it shines upon. The ship its quivering fires tincture, trembles out upon the dusk into a death-like vision; every shroud and rope is a faint line of phosphor; the canvas soars shuddering out of the sepulchral sheen and fades.

The passengers looked at one another with

stars of the blue fire in their eyes. It was just the light of horror, and just the night of quiet, with no more of the thunder left than an occasional violet glare astern to deepen to the very heart of it the meaning of that lonely flickering light away upon the sea.

A small air was stirring out of the south-west; the few stars in that quarter looked down with a shrewder tremble. The seamen were halloing about the decks as they made sail. The port-fire had burnt out. Another rocket had sailed and flashed aloft, and now the yards were being manned for the breeze, and the ship, with old Benson beside the wheel, and hands forward on the look-out for boats, was rippling softly towards the burning mass.

A dreadful fire she was when they were close enough to view her. She lighted the ocean for miles, but no boats were in sight, nor signs of living creatures aboard.

'They'll have made for the ship in the

north,' said Mr. Matthews to the second mate. And that, no doubt, was the case, though the *Queen* had been the nearer vessel. For a couple of hours old Benson kept his ship hanging in the wind, and the passengers watched with admiration and fear, a splendid but frightful picture, from which the sense of the human life that had been there, having made its escape, could not rob the spirit of tragedy. She lay but a quarter of a mile distant. Figure the tons of oil in her, the oil-soaked planks, the well-greased masts, the dripping in her every pore! The heavens overhead shook in folds of crimson to the horizon.

Captain Benson, however, was not the man to delay his voyage to enjoy a show. Four bells were struck, ten o'clock, every figure on deck had its shadow beside it, and now the moon was hanging in the sky and looking red, wild and bloated through the thick smoke that blackened the north. The skipper saw there was no life in the burning ship and no boats about; he heard four bells strike, and glancing once more at the glowing and throbbing heap which shone as daylight for anything to be seen a league round, he gave orders for sail to be trimmed. The passengers took the hint, perchance not ungratefully. They were a little weary of looking, yet they felt under an obligation to stop while the fire lasted, and the *Queen* stayed. Slowly the crimson mass drew away on the port quarter. A pleasant air was now blowing. The stars sparkled plentifully in the south and east, and the sails lifted with that look of yearning and impatience which you may notice in the ears of a horse that starts on an errand it knows. By-and-by the blaze astern was no bigger than a globular lamp glowing in the distant liquid dusk: by which hour most of the passengers, after draining their glasses or sipping wine and munching cake, had gone to bed.

Old Benson was a man of habits. When he commanded a full-rigged ship, then, in certain latitudes, he regularly took in his fore and mizzen royals and flying-jib, whether there was any occasion to do so or not; also, after the passengers had retired, and the cabin lamp was turned low, he would come on deck in his tall hat and pea coat, and smoke one Manilla cheroot, marching up and down abreast of the wheel. You might tell the time by the skipper's star of tobacco aft, and strike the bell when he threw the stump away.

He was marching up and down now, at this hour of hard upon six bells; at the forward extremity of the short white length of poop-deck stepped Mr. Poole, the second mate; a solitary figure grasped the wheel. The sails swelled to the main-royal, and from under the bows came a noise like water in little streams merrily running over shingle.

'Mr. Poole,' suddenly called out the captain in a voice that sounded harsh and parrot-like, perhaps with the suddenness of it, and the soft silence it broke into.

'Sir,' answered the second mate, and he came swiftly aft, touching his hat as he met the old skipper abreast of the after-quarter-boat, clear of the wheel.

'Whose voices are those down on the quarter-deck?'

'One's Mr. Davenire, sir. I think I hear Mr. Hankey, and there are two or three others.'

'Why don't they go to bed?'

'I don't know, sir.'

'What are they doing, sir?'

'Smoking, sir.'

After a short, expressive pause, old Benson said: 'The mate tells me you knew Mr. Hankey before he came on board this ship.'

'He came out in a ship that I was in, sir.'

'Who is he?'

'I know nothing of him, sir,' responded

the second mate, speaking nervously, as a young officer well might when challenged by a skipper in the manner which old Benson was now wearing.

'Didn't he come on board the ship the night before we sailed, at your invitation?'

'No, sir. A small boat sculled alongside. I looked over the rail and was hailed by name. Recollecting the gentleman, and understanding that he was to be a passenger aboard this ship, I asked him aboard.'

'What was your talk about?'

'Many things, sir—I forget; the ship I had come out with him in; his struggles in the colonies, and so on.'

'Did he inquire about the consignment of gold?' said the captain, standing hard as bronze upon his rounded legs, whilst he watched the face of the second mate by the light of the moon, his glowing cigar poised, a loose white hair or two trembling.

The second mate was afraid to speak the truth, and told a lie. This questioning of the old skipper astonished and alarmed him. Unformed suspicions filled his head and muddled it. When he should have said yes he answered no. The captain quitted him abruptly and went some paces forward, and strode awhile athwartship smoking, but at some feet abaft the rail at the break, so that those who stood under could not see him. There was nothing, however, for the old man to hear but a low rumble of voices, with an occasional laugh, saving that once a clearer voice began, without heed of the cuddy door being open and the ladies sleeping within, to tell a story which dismissed the old skipper to his regular post, and whilst he sucked at his cigar-end he heard a shout of laughter.

Captain Benson this night lingered a little longer than usual on deck. Seven bells found him pacing his dignity walk betwixt the wheel and the mizzen-rigging ; at this hour all was hushed under the break of the poop. The last of the passengers had turned in, and the ship was in possession of the watch on deck, who snored in corners or wearily paced the forecastle.

Now it was that old Benson, after taking a view of the compass, and sending a searching look aloft and to windward, and after gruffly delivering a sentence or two of instructions to Mr. Poole, went below to get some rest; but no man could tell at what hour this old skipper would reappear, for he was mysterious as a spectre in his tricks of emergence. Often it happened that within ten minutes of the old dog's having gone below for the night, the mate of the watch, lounging at the rail, relieved of the tyranny of that bow-legged presence, would look aft and start on beholding, walking close beside the wheel, the shadowy but familiar figure in a tall hat and long coat.

Midnight was struck on the bell, a hoarse

voice bawled down through the fore-scuttle,
' Eight bells below there ; d'ye hear the
news?' The wheel was relieved, and the
chief officer, with his eyes full of sleep, came
up the weather poop-step and talked for a
few minutes to Mr. Poole, who then went to
his cabin.

The moon was far astern on the quarter,
sinking, and the burning light of the whaler
gone long since. Clouds of fleece flew across
the stars, which shook in splendour, and
the barque strained as she drove the brine
into recoiling flashes. But the breeze had
headed her; they had braced up in that
first watch, and the ship was off her
course.

Scarcely twenty minutes had elapsed since
the watch was relieved, when Mr. Matthews,
who soberly paced the weather side of the
poop, was surprised by observing the second
mate gliding with great rapidity across the
deck from the lee poop-ladder. Matthews

came to a stand ; Mr. Poole exclaimed, breathing fast :

'What do you think? The arms-chest in my cabin has been forced, and the whole of the weapons stolen !'

CHAPTER VII

THE CAPTAIN'S STATEMENT

THE barque heeled to a damp gust of the night breeze as the second mate, in a voice low with agitation, spoke. Mr. Matthews did not rightly catch his meaning. The man repeated his words:

'All the small arms stolen out of the chest?' exclaimed Mr. Matthews, stiffening his leaning figure, and peering hard at Poole by the windy starlight. 'How long have they been gone?'

'I've only just discovered the theft,' answered the second mate.

'This must be reported to the captain at once,' said Mr. Matthews. 'Keep the deck till I return.'

He went below and knocked on the captain's door. The skipper swung in a cot, and when the mate told him that Mr. Poole had just discovered that the whole of the ship's small arms were stolen, he tumbled out of his swing bed on to the deck in shirt and drawers, as an ape drops out of a tree when shot.

'Who's done it, sir?' puffed the old man whilst he pulled on his breeches and coat, and took down his tall hat all in a passion of hurry.

'The ship must be searched for the things, sir,' said the mate.

'Ay, to her dunnage,' blew the skipper. 'The small arms stolen!' he exclaimed, brought to a halt by an instant's shock of sheer incredulity. 'Why, this looks like a plan, don't it? A conspiracy, hey, sir? Forward or aft? Softly, sir.'

He opened the door, and they stepped out lightly.

'Send Mr. Poole here,' said old Benson in a whisper like the sound of a saw, and he went straight to the second mate's cabin. He entered it without ceremony. A little lamp screwed to the bulkhead was burning. The lid of the arms-chest lay open, and the skipper had no need to look twice to see that it was empty. Whilst he was gaping at it Mr. Poole arrived.

'What's the meaning of this, sir?' said the captain, pointing to the chest.

'I have no idea, sir,' answered the second mate, who was pale and very much alarmed.

'You have the key of this chest, sir. Where is it?'

The second mate opened a locker and took out a key. 'Here it is, sir, just as I placed it. Just as it's lain from the beginning. The persons who've stolen the arms did not want my key. The lock's been forced.'

The skipper put his nose close to the heavy black chest.

'When did you make this discovery, sir?' he said, casting his little eyes about.

'Just now, sir; soon after the chief officer relieved me.'

'What made you examine the box just now?'

'The questions you put to me on deck, sir.'

'Let me see the list of the small arms.'

Mr. Poole produced a packet of papers from his little locker, and handed a dirty old parchment-like piece of stuff to the captain, who stepped close to the lamp and read aloud: 'Seven muskets, five blunderbusses, four horse-pistols, five other pistols, a dozen of cutlasses.' 'They must be in the ship,' he exclaimed. 'I don't like the look of this, sir. I'll not believe,' he went on softening his voice, with a glance at the bulkhead of the adjacent cabin, 'that the crew have had a hand in it. Yet the forecastle must be searched. This was done when all hands

were on deck, watching the whaler on fire
Who sleeps next 'e ? '

'Captain Trollope and Mr. Weston, sir.
I don't think myself——' stammered the
second mate with a bewildered look.

' What, sir, what?' panted the old skipper.

' I doubt if they're in the ship,' continued
the unfortunate officer. ' That window was
open when I came below. I don't recollect
leaving it open when I went on deck at eight
o'clock. Whoever did it has washed my
berth out for me,' and striding to his bunk
he grasped and held aloft a quantity of
blanket sodden with salt water.

The captain made no answer. He darted
many quick and curious looks around the
little interior.

Tommy Poole! Your captain viewed but
a poorly embellished hole; a portrait of
Poole's mother cut out of black paper, the
lineaments bronzed, a small crucifix at the
head of the bunk, a rack containing a few

pipes; but a man who on six pounds a month supports an old mother and a childless wife cannot handsomely furnish his cabin.

' Go and call up both stewards,' said the captain.

The two men slept in the steerage. They promptly arrived, tumbling astonished and eager out of their bunks. They were amazed to find the commander of the ship at this sepulchral hour of one bell standing hatted, his face inflamed, his hanging arms vibrating like the legs of a dreaming dog, in the cabin of the second mate, who was himself colourless as though he had been stabbed.

' Trickle,' said the captain, ' some one has plundered the arms-chest.' He pointed to it. Trickle sank his head and opened his mouth.

' Did you notice anybody hanging about the cuddy last evening when all the people were on deck looking at the fire? '

Trickle thought hard, so did John the under-steward; they stared at each other, they resolved in the anguish of their struggle with recollection; one seemed to have it, then the other with a jerk of his fist, one finger up, to no purpose. In fact, both men had been on the forecastle while the sea-show lasted, and when they went aft the passengers were coming in a body from the poop into the cuddy, talking about the fire and looking about them for grog.

Captain Benson stepped into the cuddy and moved slowly along the floor, glancing by the dimly burning lamp at the cabins to right and left of him, and at the berths in the shadow beyond the companion-steps, up which he presently stalked. He was astounded. The old heart of oak was terrified too. What could the robbery of the arms-chest signify but a conspiracy? Certain people had armed themselves at the ship's expense—for what purpose? His soul croaked a conjecture that made him reel on his sturdy bow legs as he stepped out of the hatch into the rush of the black wet wind and the gloom of the night, wild with flying cloud and dipping stars. The mate came up to him.

'The chest is plundered, sir,' panted the captain.

'Where's the ammunition, sir?' inquired the mate.

'Ha!' cried old Benson, pulling his hat down to his ears, 'I had forgotten that. Go below and tell the second mate to place the powder and ball in my cabin.'

They found the ammunition untouched. It had been stowed in the steward's pantry, and they might have hunted for it all night but for John, who, on the yesterday morning, having tumbled on his knees to explore a small cupboard for an oil-can, had handled the powder and ball without knowing what they were. They all knew that the ship carried no more ammunition than this. Mr. Matthews placed the stuff in the captain's cabin as commanded, and returned on deck to report. The old skipper was astounded.

'What's the good of muskets without powder and shot, sir?'

'Unless the people who've stolen the things brought powder and shot with them,' said the mate.

'I don't believe it,' said Captain Benson irritably. 'D'ye think it's a piece of horse-play? Some trick to scare the women? The work of one of the gentry below,' he added, turning a thumb down.

Here the second mate came up from to leeward.

'Well, sir!' exclaimed the captain.

'I'm quite sure,' said the second mate, 'that the weapons were thrown through my cabin window overboard.'

'He left his window shut and found it open when you relieved him, sir,' said the captain to the mate. 'His bed is awash

'Looks to me then like some dirty practical

joke,' said Mr. Matthews, ' and of course it will be the work of one of the ten of 'em.'

' I'd like to think so,' said the captain. ' Though it'll be a scandalous outrage at that with a rousing bill on top for the joker to pay; but better that the arms should be overboard than secreted in the ship. For what motive, sir, should a man have for breaking open an arms-chest and plundering such a collection as we carried?'

' I'd drain my heart of its blood to find out who did it, sir,' said the second mate, speaking with emotion. ' I'd give all my wages for this voyage to be able to point him out. Look at the position it puts me in, sir. You discover that I previously knew one of the passengers, and you talk to me about them in a manner that lets me see you've got your suspicions, and the next thing that happens the arms-chest in my cabin is broken open!' He added with a rising rage that forced an oath from him: 'It's enough to ruin a better man than me.'

'I have made no charges, sir,' exclaimed the captain sternly, falling back a step and riding on either leg as though he was about to spring, his custom when his anger struggled with his dignity. 'I have no doubt that things are with you precisely as they seem. You will help us to discover the people who have committed this robbery. This ship shall be thoroughly searched, Mr. Matthews, but quietly to-morrow after the cabin breakfast is over. Have you any private arms?'

'None, sir, I regret to say.'

'And you, sir?' said the skipper to Poole.

'None, sir.'

'It's not of the crew's doing,' muttered the captain, after a pause. 'There's nothing more to be said about it till daylight.'

The old man went below, but merely to look at the ammunition and stow it away. He then returned on deck, and walked it

during the rest of the night.   The mate paced
the windward planks, often sending a look
through the skylight, often pausing to bend
his ear at the companion hatch, often standing
at the brass rail forward and plunging his
sight into the deep shadows betwixt the bulwarks.   The shape of the second mate showed
shadowily to leeward.   This ship wanted a
third officer; she brought one out, but the
man, who was twenty-three years old, im-
mensely broad and a daring devil aloft, had
run with the rest at Sydney, and the captain
was unable to replace him.   The sailor at the
wheel easily saw there was something amiss,
and, on going forward when relieved at four
bells, he told his mates of the watch that the
captain was walking the deck, armed to the
teeth, that the two mates were watching likewise, and that he saw a naked revolver
swinging at Mr. Poole's fist as he passed by.
This led to some talk to leeward of the
galley.

'What the blooming blazes is wrong with the ship?' says Bob, and draining his eyes by straining them with his knuckles he stared aloft, and then around him, in the cow-like way that long-voyage sailors fall into.

'It's all right for'rads, ain't it?' said a man. 'The men are quiet enough, aren't they?'

'Perhaps the ladies are giving trouble,' exclaimed Bill.

'More likely them covies with the guffy looks and the sailor tricks—sorter drilled Jack Mucks some of 'em seem, with the shore-going togs of gents on the look-out for a job, and a general knowledge that ain't natural, 'ticklerly him with the big mays-tachianos and the cocked nose over 'em, like a duck thankin' gord for a drink. He's always a-watching of something or other, not like the rigler passenger.'

'Aft here and get a small drag upon this lee main-brace,' sang out the mate, who had

been eyeing this talking group with suspicion.

The dawn broke in a dim slate at the edge
of the working sea, flinging that tender light
of pensiveness which, as Wordsworth says,
stops just short of sadness. A melancholy
waste was the ocean till the sun flashed it up
into blue hollows and bright foam. It shone
upon three grey faces. Old Benson looked
as if he had not been to bed for a month, and
the mates as though they were just out of
jail. Poole went below to clean himself and
send his bed to the galley with the consent of
the mate whose watch it was below, and
whilst the men were washing down, the
captain called Mr. Matthews to him, and
spoke thus:

'The more I think of last night's business,
sir, the more I'm persuaded it's the work of
some of the passengers.'

'And that's my conviction.'

'I have seen nothing in the behaviour of

the men,' said the old skipper, 'to warrant suspicion of a spirit of mutiny among them.'

' Nothing, sir,' echoed the mate.

' They have not complained of the provisions, and there is nothing to find fault with in their general conduct.'

' Nothing, sir,' said Mr. Matthews, staring at the forecastle, where a seaman was making the head-pump chatter.

' I hope it may prove nothing but a practical joke,' said the captain. ' But the ship has been robbed, and the thief is aboard, and we must find him and the goods. Therefore, sir, after breakfast, you and the second mate—who is as guiltless in this thing as he says he is, the man's manner convincing—will carefully search the cabins of the passengers, and you will afterwards go forward, explain the circumstances of the robbery to the crew, and rummage the forecastle.'

' Ay, ay, sir.'

Presently Mr. Poole came on deck to take

charge of the starboard watch. The captain and the mate went below. Surely the ship was safe enough now with the glorious sun at her fore yardarm. It was a noble morning, a bright breeze, the Pacific running in long blue hills, breaking into lightning-like sea-flashes. The ship was under all the sail she needed, and smoked through the seas, shredding them at each stoop into crystal veils, which often flew in an airy beauty and a dazzling gleam of gems sheer over the forecastle head.

There was nothing in sight. The first of the passengers to come on deck was Mr. Dent. He went along to Mr. Poole, cheerfully rubbing his hands and looking about him.

'Soon up with the Horn at this rate,' he cried, 'and once round that frozen corner we shall be looking out for the north star.'

'It's a fine morning, sir,' said Mr. Poole, dryly.

Others arrived, amongst them Captain Trollope. Poole watched the tall figure of the man intently as he paced the deck seeking an appetite for his breakfast. Whilst he stared Mr. Hankey swung out of the cuddy front and came up the poop ladder.

'Good morning, Poole. I say, old man,' he said, with an insinuating leer, 'what was the shindy about last night in your cabin?'

'There was no shindy,' answered the second mate, coldly.

'A noise of voices disturbed me,' said Mr. Hankey.

'You'll often hear a noise of voices at sea,' said Poole, looking aloft with the idea of finding an excuse to sing out an order.

Mr. Hankey walked over to Captain Trollope. The breakfast bell now rang. What is more delicious to a hungry man at sea than the smell of eggs and bacon? The cuddy air was full of it, and the table was delightfully hospitable with hams, pies, boiled-beef, galley rolls, butter, yellow and sparkling with brine, and what good cheer besides? The captain came out of his cabin, the ladies assembled; in a few minutes the long table was full, the mate at the bottom, and every lee window blazed with sunshine white with foam.

'Did we make a good run in the night, captain?' said Mr. Storr.

'Yes, sir,'

'You were a good deal about, weren't you, captain?' said Mrs. Peacock. 'I heard your voice.'

'The sea's an up and down life, madam,' answered the old skipper.

'That girl opposite is taking us all in,' said Johnson, with his eyes on his plate, to Davenire.

'Which of us would she choose if the chance were hers?' answered Davenire with a cool smile as he met the fine eyes of Miss Mansel.

'Were you disturbed by the shindy last

night, Mr. Matthews?' said Hankey, calling down the table, whilst he cut himself a slice of ham.

'Shindy's a strong word,' answered the mate, with a troubled look and a glance at the skipper. 'Is it English?'

'What took place in the night?' said Captain Trollope.

The mate seemed to be listening to what Mr. Dent was saying; the merchant talked of wool and horns, the prosperity of the colony, and the duties of the mother country. Conversation trickled on down both sides of the table, till, breakfast being nearly over, Mr. Isaac Cavendish started up. Instantly Captain Benson shot out of his chair, and grasping the table, his face discoloured by twenty passions and feelings, he cried out, 'I request that nobody will quit the cuddy till I have made a statement.'

A deep silence followed this. All the people stared. Mrs. Peacock turned of a

dead white; Mrs. Storr seized her husband's
arm; Mr. Cavendish sat down, and every
face on either hand the table was directed at
the captain. Mr. Matthews quickly and
keenly glanced at some of the men. Their
faces expressed simple wonder and great
curiosity tinctured with expectation of amusement. Captain Trollope pulled his moustache
whilst he watched the skipper; in fact, his
face sat almost expressionless behind that
abundant decoration.

'I hope no needless alarm will attend
what I'm going to say—I refer to you ladies'—
began the old white-haired man very purple,
very agitated. 'This ship carries an arms-
chest containing weapons for the defence of
the people aft in case of trouble forward, or
in case of any other difficulty,' he added,
stuttering on spunkily, with a look at Trollope
such as he would direct at a black squall he
couldn't see through. 'The chest was in the
second mate's cabin; the lock has been

smashed, and the whole of the weapons removed.'

Mr. Storr's jaw fell.

'With what object?' asked Mr. Dent, endeavouring to speak as though he felt perfectly cool.

'We don't know, sir. But what we certainly do know is the thief is in the ship.'

'At which end of her do you imagine, Captain Benson?' asked Captain Trollope coldly and haughtily.

'We shall find out, sir,' responded the skipper, speaking with fifty marks of dislike and suspicion of the man.

'But good gracious, captain, are we in danger?' said Mrs. Holroyd.

'In no danger whatever, madam.'

'Do you suspect anybody?' called out Mr. Masters, jerking the words at the captain with a petulance that was like insolence.

'The lock smashed, d'ye say?' exclaimed Mr. Storr. 'That would have made a noise.

Who heard such a noise ? ' He advanced his head and looked up and down the table.

' It was done when everybody was on deck last night watching the fire,' said the captain.

' Is it some sleep-walker's trick ? ' exclaimed Mr. Caldwell in his sulkiest manner.

' What do you think ? ' cried Mr. Dent, catching at the fancy and staring eagerly.

' There's Burn here who talks and sings in his sleep,' exclaimed Mr. Davenire, ' but I don't know that he walks. D'ye walk, Burn ? '

' It would be horrible to believe it,' exclaimed Mrs. Peacock, looking at the fat man.

' I walk in my sleep, but I've not done this,' said Mr. Shannon.

' I am sorry to have to tell you, ladies and gentlemen,' here broke in the captain roughly, ' that, in the interests of the lives and property committed to my charge, every passenger's berth must be thoroughly searched.'

'The ladies?' said Mr. Weston in a small voice, looking, with his wrung face, as though after speaking he thrust his tongue in his cheek.

'I said every cabin, sir,' thundered the captain.

'Quite welcome to begin with mine,' said Captain Trollope sarcastically. 'If I can be of any help—perhaps some of us here may have been forced by circumstances into the Excise—you have a custom house in Sydney, hey?' he called across to Mr. Dent, who made no reply.

'So far as I am concerned,' said Mr. Cavendish, smirking at the skipper, 'I'm quite willing that my cabin should be searched. But wouldn't it show some breeding, captain, and that sort of courtesy which fifty and sixty guineas may be thought money enough to purchase, if you began with the forecastle?'

He bowed and sat back with his repellent, incommunicable look of self-complacency.

'I assure you there's no need to search *my* cabin,' said Mrs. Holroyd.

Some laughter crackled in the neighbourhood of the mate, who listened to what was passing with a dark face and fixed attention.

'I am very sorry, ladies,' said the skipper bluntly, 'that you should have been brought into such a matter as this aboard my ship. Very sorry.' He bowed to them in a general way. 'We must find out who's robbed the arms-chest, and what's become of the weapons. Since, then, the cabins *must* be searched, this atrocious piece of rascality,' he added, scowling into the air, 'was bound to reach your ears, exaggerated, of course. I hope,' he went on, gazing significantly at the row of faces on either hand, 'that there is no gentleman here who objects to his cabin being searched?'

'You may search away for me. Begin at

once. The forecastle should show the road though in such a job.' These and the like exclamations followed the captain's remark.

' You don't open portemanteaux, I hope ? ' said Captain Trollope, and he glowed as he spoke.

' That I shouldn't permit,' said Mr. Davenire, with a mounting colour handsomely managed.

'We must find the weapons, gentlemen,' exclaimed the captain. ' I am speaking in the interests of the ship and of our lives.'

Saying this, he left the table, fetched his hat, and went on deck. The mate followed. The passengers remained seated, talking.

' What's the meaning of it all ? ' exclaimed Mrs. Peacock.

' I should like to see the chest,' said Mr. Johnson. ' Suppose the lock smashed, *that's* no warrant the box ever contained small arms.'

' I doubt if the master of a vessel has a

right to search his passengers' cabins,' exclaimed Captain Trollope, sitting with a lofty air, 'though Captain Benson's welcome to begin with mine, as I told him.'

'The powers of a commander of a ship are absolutely despotic,' said Mr. Dent. 'They are unlimited, and very properly so.'

'But who the deuce wants to steal a ship's small arms?' exclaimed Mr. Burn with a grin as he ran his eyes over the people opposite. 'Were these arms valuable? Were they choicely mounted? Were they precious on the score of antiquity? Pah!' said he, with a shrug, standing up, 'you'll find there's been some stupid blunder. The arms were never stowed perhaps, and perhaps the second mate never noticed until last night that the lock was smashed when the box was shipped.'

He rolled down the cuddy and on to the quarter-deck, where he filled a pipe.

'He talks too much,' lightly groaned

Captain Trollope in Mr. Davenire's ear, as they followed the fat man.

The people quitted the table. Some entered their cabins as though to await the persons who were to search them. Four or five men got together on the quarter-deck close against the cabin front, and stood smoking; of these first one and then another in a careless, offhand way would go to their cabins, then return, lighting their pipes afresh. The seamen had not been put to work; they hung in a little crowd abreast of the galley, looking aft with countenances of expectation. It was clear that one of the mates had gone forward, told the crew what had happened, and they waited for the forecastle to be rummaged.

Old Benson walked the deck with a resolved gait and as stern an expression as the hearty looks of his face could put on. He reasoned with himself thus, and his lips worked as he discoursed to his own heart:

'If some of those gentry have plundered the arms-chest and distributed the weapons amongst them, they may throw them overboard through their cabin windows before the search begins. I am in no hurry therefore, for I want *that* to happen. Better that the things should be hove through the windows than secreted, or even a portion of them secreted. If they are secreted it is with a design, and that design——'

The horror of the fancy forced him into a quick walk, and the helmsman grinned to see how the white-haired old man talked to himself.

Both mates were on deck. Somebody struck four bells, ten o'clock. Mr. Storr came on to the poop with his wife on his arm. Miss Mansel also arrived: presently Caldwell, Johnson, and Hankey lounged up the poop ladder from the quarter deck. The captain on seeing them called to Mr. Matthews:

'Begin the search, sir, and take Mr. Poole with you.'

Whilst these words were still in the skipper's mouth Captain Trollope rose through the companion way and stepping across to old Benson, he exclaimed somewhat stiffly, carrying himself with a well-bred air, 'If I can help your officers in searching this ship, pray command me.'

'We shall be glad of whatever assistance the passengers render us,' said Captain Benson, standing bolt upright with his arms hanging down.

'It is inconceivable,' said Captain Trollope, 'that this theft or joke, as it may turn out, should be the work of anybody aft.'

'We must find that out, sir,' answered the skipper bluntly, and to rid himself of the gentleman he stepped to the binnacle stand and watched his ship from beside it.

One of the most extraordinary incidents that ever occurred on the high seas followed.

CHAPTER VIII

THE SEARCH

THE mates left the poop together: the passengers who were then on deck followed them, and old Benson stumped his three fathoms of white plank alone. The seamen grouped near the galley were now talking with some excitement. Old Benson looked nervous and disordered in spirits as he glanced at the open skylights. That he was within his rights in searching the passengers' berths he hoped rather than knew. There were not many marine Acts of Parliament in those days. Benson feared trouble on his arrival in England—detaining law-suits which might imperil his command. Was he wise, moreover, he wondered, in rendering his suspicions peculiarly significant by ordering the cuddy to be attacked before the forecastle ?

He stepped uneasily along on his short arched legs, red and troubled, a singular little figure of a seaman, almost shapeless with his hat down to his ears and his broad beam of coat. There were commanders at sea that morning in cheerfuller spirits than Captain Benson.

Meanwhile they had begun to search the cuddy. Mr. Matthews did not like the job, neither did Mr. Poole. Both men had frankly looked their apologies in a sailorly way, and most of the company understood their feelings.

'Is it not reasonable,' exclaimed Captain Trollope advancing from the companion stairs to the cuddy front as the two mates entered, and thus arresting them, so to speak, on the very threshold of their business, ' that we should be satisfied first of all that there *is* a chest of weapons broken open ? '

'But even then,' said Mr. Caldwell, 'are we to believe that there were arms in it?'

'Gentlemen,' said the mate, 'you shall see the chest.'

He opened the door of Mr. Poole's berth. Several persons entered; two or three others talked at the table apparently without interest in what was passing. The ladies kept their cabins.

'Now you see it,' said the mate.

Hankey examined the lock and exclaimed 'Yes, newly smashed, by Jove! no doubt of that.'

The second mate lifted the lid, and Captain Trollope, looking down into the open box over his folded arms, said, 'What were the weapons?'

'Blunderbusses, horse-pistols, cutlasses, and so on,' said Poole, scarcely able to hold his face as he gave a name to the ridiculous parcel.

The mates were half stunned by the roar of laughter that attended this.

'Good booty!' exclaimed Captain Trollope, wiping his lips. He burst into another laugh. 'Blunderbusses and horse-pistols, eh! I think I see old Captain Benson taking aim: the wrong eye shut—a purple face glowing at the butt-end like the August moon at the tail of a shoal, the piece all trigger and the flint gone.'

Another shout of laughter.

'Suppose we begin the search *here*,' said Mr. Davenire, looking with crooked eyebrows at the portrait of Poole's mother, whilst Mr. Caldwell advanced his black head to view the crucifix.

The mate looked a remonstrance. He did not relish the officiousness of these gentlemen. But he had overheard the skipper's answer to Captain Trollope on the poop, and had nothing to say. The search then began. The locker was opened, the mattress tumbled, they peered under the bunk, they beat the bulkheads as though for secret panels and mysterious hiding-places.

They next went in a body to the mate's berth. Ten gentlemen were now assisting the two officers to find the plunder, and they made a considerable crowd in the little cabin. Their number was a trouble : nothing could be done for elbows and shoving.

'There's no good in all this skylarking,' said Burn; 'I mean if the thief's to be discovered.'

'There's nothing here,' said Captain Trollope, looking around him with slight disdain over the head of the mate.

'Bet your holiest prospects on *that*,' said Mr. Matthews slowly, cap in hand, wiping his face, for indeed the whole of them shone with perspiration and most of them with good spirits.

'Next cabin,' shouted Mr. Masters, and the heaped dashed in a huddle into the cuddy bearing the two mates helpless in the thick of them.

'Aren't you going to search the ship with us?' bawled Mr. Hankey to Mr. Storr, who stood in a posture of uncertainty at the head of the table. The little auctioneer responded with a pale smile, and a weak meaningless flourish of the hand.

'There's the captain looking!' said Shannon in a low voice to Caldwell, and they both laughed. Sure enough in the open frame of the skylight was the head of the skipper: he gazed down with his face full of blood, amazed and enraged, but he, like his officer, had nothing to say.

The next cabin attacked was the one shared between Mr. Dike Caldwell and Mr. Isaac Cavendish. The twelve filled this little room like a burst of wind. There was hardly space for an elbow to jerk itself. Shouts of laughter reached the captain's ears; they tumbled the mattress, they roared over an old razor strop. A tooth-brush was flung through the open port-hole: it was Caldwell's, and he turned savagely upon the joker.

'That portmanteau?' said the mate.

'No, you don't,' said Caldwell, with one of his ugly black scowls; and he sat down upon it.

'Mr. Matthews, I appeal to your common sense,' exclaimed Captain Trollope, endeavouring to fan himself with his hat: 'is it conceivable, even supposing Mr. Caldwell were the culprit, that he'd thrust the rusty contents of an old arms-chest among his shirts and waistcoats?'

'You don't touch it,' snarled Mr. Caldwell, keeping his seat and looking dangerously at the mate. 'Not that your rotten stuff *is* here,' he added, smiting the leather: 'but they've thrown my tooth-brush away, and I'll be hanged if these gentlemen shall make a fool of me by a public exhibition of my private effects.'

'It was understood that the portemanteaux were not to be touched,' said Mr. Davenire.

'It's a measly business so far as I am concerned, gentlemen,' said the mate, 'something new to me in this line of life. I don't fancy' he added dryly, 'that we shall find the weapons we want in these cabins.'

'Obey orders, if you break owners,' said Mr. Weston. 'Next cabin and shove ahead.'

Thus they proceeded, and the captain meanwhile came and went at the skylight. It was noticeable that the men contrived that their own cabins should be first searched; they rushed the business with the mates by help of laughter, skylarking, and crowding. When it came to the ladies' cabins, however, there was a well-mannered pause.

'The mates may now search for themselves,' said Captain Trollope, twisting on his heel; and, pulling out a cigar case, he strolled contemptuously and leisurely towards the quarter-deck.

'Trollope,' shouted Hankey, 'the captain's cabin hasn't been searched yet.'

'By thunder, no!' cried Trollope, coming hastily back to the group.

'You'll not enter my cabin, if you please,' roared the captain through the skylight.

'Captain Benson,' said Mr. Davenire, going under the skylight and looking up through an eyeglass, 'you have affronted us, the first-class passengers of the *Queen*, with your suspicions. We now *choose*,' he went on with a well-contrived drawl, 'to suspect *you* of having plundered the arms-chest.'

The skipper looked down with the spirit of murder aflame in each deep-seated little eye. He was dumb with wrath till, finding his voice, he shouted to Mr. Matthews to come on deck. Some of the men were then for going at once to the captain's cabin; Trollope restrained them.

'We'll do better than that,' said he;

'we'll get a red herring of apology out of him for the trail.'

'Gentlemen,' said the mate, coming down the companion steps after a few minutes, 'by order of the captain the search is over. Follow me to the fo'c'sle, Mr. Poole.'

'I say,' here bawled Mr. Johnson, 'aren't Mr. Dent and Mr. Storr's cabins to be searched?'

'The innocence of us all aft,' said the mate with a grave smile, 'has converted the whole thing into a joke. The captain's desire is that it may go no further.'

'A joke!' growled Mr. Caldwell, pushing his scowling face close to the mate, whose fists instantly doubled, whilst his smile fled like a shadow of cloud from his features; 'you search my cabin as if I was a thief, and you call it a joke.'

'It's you who've made a joke of it: I was obeying orders,' exclaimed the mate, with a slight shade of green entering his complexion as he looked round him.

'The culprit is the commander, not his officers, Caldwell,' said Captain Trollope.

' Cheer up, Poole,' said Hankey, slapping the second mate on the back ; 'jump forward now, and carry the mate along with you ; it's the sailor who hopped overboard that's the thief, and you'll find the whole of the weapons in his sea-boots.'

Mr. Dent came out of his cabin and stood with Mr. Storr.

' I say,' exclaimed Captain Trollope, striding up to them with an unlighted cigar in his hand, ' we mean to make the skipper apologise for this affront. You expect an apology, I suppose?'

' The captain is within his rights—I don't wish to meddle—where are the firearms?' answered Mr. Storr, stammering with un-easiness.

Captain Trollope looked down at him

with so inimitable a countenance of anger
and disgust that the little man trembled.

'Come on deck,' said Mr. Dent; and the
two men climbed the companion steps.

The ladies now came forth. Mr. Burn
officiously offered his arm to Mrs. Dent, who
declined with the curtsey of a cook. Mrs.
Peacock was conducted up the steps by Mr.
Hankey; the other ladies helped themselves.
They were briskly followed by the ten gentlemen, with Captain Trollope at their head. It
was hard upon noon, and the captain was
calling through the skylight to the steward
for his sextant. Forward the ship looked
deserted. In fact the mess kids had been
carried from the galley, and the men ate their
dinner whilst the two mates went the rounds
of Jack's sea-parlour.

This was the situation at this hour. The
captain was about to take sights, and the ten
knew their business too well to hinder him.
They lounged until eight bells had been

made, the old skipper sharing his fiery
glances between them and the sun, and
when the bell was being struck by a seaman who smoked furtively whilst he stood
waiting, the two mates came out of the forecastle.

'Let's hear the report,' murmured Trollope to Davenire.

Mr. Matthews, followed by Poole, came
on to the poop; he was pale with heat,
perhaps with fatigue; he was scarcely recovered from an illness, and the corners of
his mouth drooped with dislike and contempt
of his latest job. The ladies and most of the
men crowded close to hear. Most of the
women looked very frightened. Miss Mansel's
dark pensive eyes were frequently directed
in rapid glances at some of the gentlemen.
The little skipper stood bolt upright, his arms
hanging, his sextant in his clutch at his side.
The mates touched their caps.

'Well, sir?' said Captain Benson.

'We can find nothing that answers to what's missing,' said Mr. Matthews.

'I never believed that the weapons *were* forward,' said the little skipper, rosy with rising wrath.

'Captain Benson,' exclaimed Captain Trollope, towering up close to him—Dent and Storr shrinking to see it, though the mates instantly put themselves on either hand their captain—'that sentence, sir, was far from well in your mouth after what has occurred. But let that be as it will; I, together with other gentlemen here, expect that you will make us—the whole of your passengers, in short—an abundant apology for the affront you have put upon us.'

'As how?' sputtered the captain, starting back with a paralytic flourish of his sextant. 'I am commander of this ship. The vessel has been plundered of her arms. Where are they? Can you tell me?' he cried, making a hideous face at Captain Trollope, with his sneer of vehement scorn that opened his lips and almost eclipsed his familiar countenance with wrinkles and terrifying looks. 'I suppose, as a passenger, you have an interest in the safety of the vessel? I take it,' he began to roar, looking with real fury around him, but always at the gentlemen, 'that *you* must wish, equally with myself and your fellow-passengers, to discover the thieves, that we may judge of their motives. Apologise! I'd sooner sink the ship.'

'Oh, gentlemen!' shrieked Mrs. Peacock, 'what are you exciting the captain like this for?'

'For mercy's sake don't think of sinking the ship,' whined Mrs. Holroyd, clutching her daughter by the arm; and both their faces were as white as any sail above them.

'If you don't apologise,' said Captain Trollope, 'you will hear of us again on your arrival.'

'If you persist in this conduct, sir,' ex-

claimed Captain Benson, scowling up heroi-
cally into Trollope's face, 'I'll have you laid
by the heels—I'll have you in irons as a
mutineer—you shall know my power as commander, by——' And this little man who
never swore made his speech awful to the
ladies with an oath.

Captain Trollope turned a deep scarlet;
he stood motionless, but speechless also;
others of the ten men bit their lips and
looked towards the bows; Caldwell drew
closer to the captain by a stealthy pace, and
a face that made Mr. Storr feel sick. The
crew were watching and listening. They had
gradually drifted in a body to abreast of the
main hatchway, and were still coming aft.
No man in his senses could have mistaken
their attitude. Was it this, or quite another
reason, that caused Captain Trollope to walk
suddenly over to leeward, where he overhung
the rail, gazing seawards, and swinging one
foot in hard kicks against a stanchion?

The skipper stood watching him for a minute or so; his lips worked. It looked as though he would be unable to restrain some command that raged like a choking fire in his throat. Then suddenly exclaiming, 'Mr. Matthews, turn the men to, sir. Let the business of the ship go on, then attend me in my cabin. Mr. Poole, you'll keep the lookout,' he stepped to the companion way and vanished.

The records of forecastle mutiny form probably about two-thirds of marine literature. But who ever heard of a revolt amongst the first-class passengers of a ship? There is one memorable instance, indeed, of an officer in command of a number of soldiers causing the captain to be clapped in irons, and thus degraded, the unhappy seaman was carried to St. Helena, the ship being navigated by the mate, at the point of the bayonet. The theft of the small arms, the insults, the behaviour of ten at least of the passengers looked uncommonly like the dark shadow of mutiny, or some bitter bloody trouble of a similar sort at hand —but *aft!*

The mate having turned the men to, and taken a look at the ship's course, entered the captain's cabin. The old skipper, reverend with white hair, and comely with the look of sailorly heartiness and manliness which his hat half hid when it clothed his forehead to the white line of his eyebrows, stood at his little table with a hand upon it, lost in thought. He started when the mate entered, and instantly looked stern and full of business.

'You found nothing forward, of course, sir? I can judge by the deportment of the crew that they are to be trusted. Some one aft has robbed the ship; more than one perhaps; what has he done with the weapons? What was his object in stealing them?'

'We have the powder and ball, sir,' said the mate. 'If they're aboard, the things are as useless as if they were over the side.'

'Who is that Captain Trollope? Who are these ten passengers? They are a confederacy, sir. They threaten mischief—what do they intend?'

'I believe, sir,' said the slow and practical mate, viewing his captain's inflamed face with steadfast thoughtful eyes, 'that you will discover this business is nothing more than a practical joke, poor and vulgar, but something to make a bankrupt of its author if he's to be come at. Mr. Poole in the fo'c'sle told me this, recollecting the matter with a sudden surprise. He said the gentleman named Hankey, during his visit to the ship the night before we sailed, asked, among other questions, about the arms-chest, and burst into a laugh when the box was shown him and the contents stated.'

'Stated—stated!' blew the little man in a great fit of passion; 'what right had the second officer to *state* the contents as you call it, to receive a visitor, to talk to him, I say? Was he drunk?'

'Looks to me, sir, as if Mr. Hankey was the prime joker in this job.'

'Who's to prove it?' hissed the fiery skipper. 'His cabin was searched, I suppose?'

'No man of that ten is fool enough to hide two or three hundredweight of old iron and steel in his cabin with the stewards in and out and the stuff itself plunder, sir.'

'Is the second officer to be trusted? Give me reason to doubt him, and I'll break him out of hand; he shall be under lock and key for the rest of the voyage.'

The mate reflected and answered earnestly, 'You'll find he's perfectly honest and trust-worthy, sir.'

'You don't forget what we're carrying home, do 'e?'

'I do not,' answered the mate firmly.

'Give the men to understand that we have our suspicions of the ten cuddy passengers, and start them on keeping a bright look-out for themselves. Let them know it may come to their saving their throats by doing it.'

The mate, with astonishment slowly growing in his face, said 'Ay, ay, sir. But what name and shape am I to give to our suspicions?'

The old skipper was at a loss. He stared vacantly through the large cabin window, then exclaimed, 'We must watch 'em. You will keep your eye upon 'em, sir. You will keep your eye upon Mr. Poole also.'

They stood thus in somewhat aimless discourse for another ten minutes or so. The mate then left the cabin.

Though there was plenty of white flying sunshine and sparkling weather overhead, a gloom dark as the shadow of storm lay upon the people when they sat at lunch that day. From time to time Captain Trollope would

sternly look at the skipper, and the skipper
would return the look with equal sternness,
and to a spiritual eye with the word 'Irons'
writ large upon his face. If people spoke, it
was scarcely more than to ask for things.
Mrs. Peacock, it is true, once inquired if the
thief had been discovered, but the answer she
got silenced her, and Mr. Dent and Mr. Storr
were afraid to mention the subject.

However, tiffin at sea is no detaining meal,
and the chairs fore and aft were quickly emptied; the captain called the steward, went to
his cabin, and there questioned the man
closely; he had faith in this fellow. His
name was Trickle, he was legged like his
master, and was about thirty years old, and
the Jacks would tell him he walked on his
father's legs, and it was right the skipper
should take a fatherly interest in him. He
had nothing to tell the commander of the
ship; had no suspicions. He was of Mr. Matthews's opinion; that it was a practical joke,

with some deeper meaning in it than fooling, as for instance it might have been the work of one who disliked the second mate and hoped to get him into trouble.

'Go and send the second mate to me.'

Poole was eating his lunch in the chief mate's place. He arose nervously.

'So it seems, sir,' let fly old Benson in a broadside of sputters the instant the young fellow presented himself, 'that you did not give me the whole truth when I questioned you about your knowledge of some of the passengers.'

'I told you all I then recollected, sir.'

'Did you tell me that you had shown the arms-chest and stated its contents to the gentleman named Hankey when he visited the ship in Sydney Bay?'

'I forgot all about that, sir. I am heartily sorry. God knows I'd have stove his boat in sooner than have allowed him aboard could I have foreseen this.'

Benson's passion rose high; he thundered and swelled. 'D'ye know what my power as commander is, sir?'

'Too well,' sighed Poole, standing upright like a private.

'How am I to know you're not in league with certain people in this ship for some purpose that I mean to watch and frustrate, sir? D'ye know your responsibilities? If I catch ——'

His speech was arrested by a sensation of choking; it was over in a minute, but the second mate was greatly alarmed, and asked if he should procure some brandy. The skipper waved aside the question with a stout-hearted flourish of his arm, and was about to speak when he was again halted by his eyes lighting upon the barometer close past the second mate.

'That will do, sir,' and the officer left the cabin.

The commander, whose face had recovered

its wonted hue, opened a locker and drank a
glass of liquor. He then looked at the barometer again, critically considering the fall,
which was indeed of a character to demand
his earnest attention. He put on his hat and
went on deck, and, without noticing anybody,
stepped to the wheel, looked at the course,
then at sea and sky, then aloft at his ship.

It was hard upon ten o'clock. The ocean
swept blue from the ship to the southern
horizon, where it ran fretting in a queer tinge
of olive that was as though a dye of storm
were sifting and spreading into the brine from
far recesses down the slope. But the breeze
was fresh, the sea ran in brilliance, the ship
rushed in foam, and there was nothing in the
heavens or the waters to indicate an approach-
ing change.

The gloom of the cabin, however, was
upon the poop just the same. The passengers
conversed in low voices, and when the captain
made his appearance the ladies silently

watched him. All healthy spirit of comrade-ship had been broken up amongst the mates; you saw Captain Trollope lounging in the gangway leaning against the bulwarks, stern and lonely. Shannon squatted solitary upon the grating abaft the wheel till the captain emerged, when darting an ugly look at the old skipper, he slouched forwards, keeping alone, however. So with the rest, saving Burn and Masters, who sat together diverting them-selves, the one with working a Turk's head upon a piece of rope, the other watching him.

That afternoon, some while before eight bells, a film drew over the sky, it was laden with a delicate beading of cloud; in places it looked like netting. The sun lost shape and flooded twice his diameter with an oozing or draining of sickly light. The sails of the ship took an odd sulky glare of brass, and there being little wind they sucked hard into the masts at every roll upon the mountain swell out of the south.

The glass had continued to fall. There was storm in the face of the heavens, in the weedy swells of the sea. The sun went out in a blood-red smoky glare, and the night fell, black as ink, with a light air out of the eastward and a wild moan in each gust, which the heavy dip of the ship on the large swell forced betwixt her masts. But long ere this she had been snugged down to a few cloths of canvas; full of savage beauty was the picture she made when having rounded into the trough she rolled her naked spars athwart that sullen flare of sunset in the far north-west.

The gale grew slowly. It sprang out of the blackness and filled the rigging with a hundred piercing whistles. It had an edge of antarctic spite in it, and for the cold of that first low blast there might have been a continent of ice close aboard. It freshened. The lashed seas split in thunder-claps against the diving and straining ship, and the darkness was made a visible whiteness by the foam that burst off bow and beam. At two in the morning it was blowing a hurricane. The sea was running in black hills, and the face of it was frightful with the light of the storm. The slant of the deck at each leeward roll was steep as a roof, the helmsmen were lashed to their posts. The captain stood under the shelter of a square of canvas in the mizzen rigging belted to belaying pins. The mate hung to leeward where the pitiless shriek and roar sometimes flew high enough above his head to yield him the sensation of a lull.

In the grey of the morning the wind slackened, yet it still blew a living gale. The discomfort was shocking. The main-deck was drowned and the cuddy awash spite of the secured doors. The ladies lay in their beds speechless with sickness and terror. Mr. Dent, with clenched teeth, wrote an account of their condition and thrust the paper into a bottle which he carefully corked, then with reeling head and flying legs he gained the companion steps, rose upon them to the height of his head, and watching his chance, flung the bottle at the sea with such dexterity that it struck the rail and went to splinters upon the deck, at the instant that his wideawake flew cleverly overboard. The captain, holding by the rigging, and leaning in his girdle like a man heaving the lead, roared some words into the wind at the colonial merchant, who, catching no meaning and fearing for his life if he trusted to his legs, slided down into the cuddy and regained his cabin.

This happened shortly before the breakfast hour. The ship was then labouring heavily and the stewards prepared a meal at the risk of their lives; they were constantly thrown; they stumbled, and tripped, and reeled with their hands full of crockery. Some of the ten emerged and cheerfully helped them. By the time breakfast was ready the whole of the ten gentlemen had left their cabins and were seating themselves in their accustomed places as the old skipper came below.

Giving his spray-soaked hat to one of the stewards, he took his chair at the head of the table. Some of the gentlemen catching his eye bowed. He inclined his head gravely, and inquired of the steward after the ladies and Mr. Dent and Mr. Storr. They wanted nothing, he was answered. The name of food increased their nausea. Mr. Hankey and two or three others seemed desirous by the looks they cast at the captain to propitiate him. Captain Trollope sat grim and hard-faced as a figure-head. It was something dark, however, down here; a single lamp was burning; the shadow of the flying sky lay like a thin fading coating of some grey paint upon the skylights; at intervals a brightness of foam was flashed inwards through the weather windows, but to leeward the glass lay almost continuously buried deeper than the thunderous dazzle went, and the atmosphere that way was charged with the dusky green of the sea.

The table submitted a poor show of dishes ; the cook could do nothing with the galley fire, and the ten gentlemen and Captain Benson— the mate did not appear—drank beer or wine.

'It blows a strong gale of wind, sir,' said Mr. Johnson politely ; he sat nearest to the captain.

'It blows hard, sir,' answered old Benson, arresting the hand with which he was about to cut a slice of some kind of sausage, whilst he watched the steward crawl on his hands and feet to leeward to pick up a piece of ship's beef that had sprung from the table.

'I presume there is no danger?' said Mr. Masters.

The captain let his little eyes dwell upon the man for a minute ; he then answered with a significant look, with one of those slips which will make old-fashioned English of old men's talk, 'Was you never at sea before?'

'Oh, just a little,' answered Mr. Masters airily, but with a mind of caution that betrayed itself in the fingers he fiddled his tumbler of beer with ; 'but I was never in such a hurricane as this.'

'Gentlemen,' said the old skipper firmly, 'you are all of you very fortunate in possessing good sea legs. There are not many landsmen who could sit and eat at this table with so much courage and good spirits, and with so nice a trick of fitting themselves to the heave.'

Captain Trollope looked hard at him, but did not speak.

'Mr. Cavendish,' called out Burn, 'you for one, I think, have knocked about amongst ships?'

Mr. Cavendish answered with a pleasant nod over a glass of foaming ale.

'Others of these gentlemen, so far as I have been able to gather,' continued Mr. Burn, motioning in a gentlemanlike way, 'have tasted of the perils to which your life is wedded. In these times men see and do much.'

'I believe so, sir,' answered the captain with a grunt of suspicion, choking further words, however, with a mouthful of sausage.

'I presume, sir,' said Mr. Caldwell, turning his gloomy face upon the captain, 'that you don't begrudge me the privilege of sitting at this table in a gale of wind merely because I happen to enjoy what you think proper to call a pair of sea-legs?'

'Certainly not, sir, certainly not,' responded the captain, swallowing at the risk of suffocation to get the words out quickly. 'I am always happy to see my passengers assembled at table, and I wish the ladies were with us this morning,' and he rolled a somewhat vacant eye upon the cabins abreast.

After this no man spoke for some time. The long pause was filled with the dull thunder of shattering seas. The cabin was loud with the shrieks and groans of strained fastenings. The roaring in the rigging sank in a giant tremble through the shaft of mizzenmast, and shook the interior like the vibrations of an engine. In momentary trances when the ship lay rail under in the deep hollow—in those breathless moments ere she was rushed to the height of the green acclivity that flickered mountainous on her bow like flashes of lightning before thundering into white water, you heard the dim beat of the rudder, the furious drag of it at the wheel chains.

The ten gentlemen ate and drank silently, but with calmness. They conveyed their wants by pantomime, and helped one another with well-bred alacrity, yet as though the novelty of acquaintance was not wholly worn off. Little Benson took mental notes of these and other points. The plain sailor was astonished. Could these ten gentlemanly men of various ages be the—the what? Ay, *that* was it. He munched and was bewildered.

All of a sudden Captain Trollope, standing

up but holding on, addressed Captain Benson in a huge, hurricane-lunged voice such as a man would send across a moor at night for help : ʻYou have had time to reflect, sir, and now probably you will see your way to make the voyage a pleasant one by apologising for the affront you caused your mates to put upon us yesterday.ʼ

The skipper jumped up and looked at him ; his lips worked, but no sound was made ; then, with a gesture of frenzy, he hoisted his arm and snapped his fingers at Captain Trollope. In this strange posture he remained for some time, swaying on his arched legs like a swing-tray, watched by some of the men as though he had gone out of his mind. He then called for his hat, drew it to his ears, and again snapping his fingers at Captain Trollope, stepped on deck.

A great laugh went up when the little chap passed out, and no man's laugh was louder than Trollope's.

CHAPTER IX

OVERHEARD

THE *Queen* struggled with this violent weather for six days. It was in the teeth of her course, and blew her north-north-west above a hundred leagues. She was nothing strained in the hold; her pumps sucked after a brief spell; but aloft she showed a distressed look, with the rain-blackened canvas frapped to the yards and the gear blowing out slack as a man-of-war's pennon in a light wind.

The roaring outside, however, subdued all life within. The captain and mate would occasionally talk over the robbery of the arms-chest; but the gale and the safety of the ship were overwhelming present anxieties, and the incident of the theft grew dim as a fact and as a dangerous riddle. Likewise the captain gave but scant attention to the ten. They loafed through the furious weather as best they could, snugging down in corners for a smoke and markedly breaking themselves up, so that they seemed no longer the same company of gentlemanly men who had come together by chance and quickly developed into a gang-like clan. They'd come on deck, and, holding on stoutly, stare for a little into the whole heart of the blast. Then the captain, aswing in his hempen belt under the shelter of a square of canvas, would watch them. Some seemed to like to test their power of eye and strength of breath by thus facing what they were bound speedily to turn their backs upon. Of these were that massive man with the silver chain, Mark Davenire, and, strangely enough, the fat Mr. Burn.

That most of them had used the sea professionally no one could doubt; nothing but custom could have made the wild hull of the

Queen so easy to their legs. The mate seemed more struck by this than by the plunder of the arms-chest, or by the captain's suspicions of the people and his behaviour to Captain Trollope. He paused once to exchange a few sentences with Poole: the commander was below, and they stood in the shelter of the canvas in the mizzen rigging, where they could hear each other.

'Look at that man,' says Mr. Matthews, gazing askew at Mr. Peter Johnson, who stood with two others at the break of the poop, holding by the rail; 'he's been a soger in his day. *Must* have been! What but a drill sergeant could have straightened his spine so? Yet call me the thief of the chest if he hasn't been a sailor too. Where's his shell-back, then? Why isn't he curved like the rest of us?'

'Wasn't long enough at it perhaps, sir,' answers Poole.

'They're watching this ship,' continued

the mate, ' as seamen would. The fat chap asked me why we hadn't sent down our royal yards. Why didn't we rig our flying jibboom in and send down the long topgallant-masts? He said he and some of the others would lend the sailors a hand if the thing was urgent.'

'Well, I'm jiggered!' exclaimed Poole with a kind of admiration in his faint smile.

'I don't know,' the mate went on, ' if the captain's made any observations. I've logged a few fancies down in my mind whilst watching them this weather. It seems to me that they come up to study the ship. I saw Mr. Shannon with that black devil Caldwell at his elbow. It was yesterday morning: they stood as those three are now standing, and I've gone dark and see only a madman's sights if the beggar Shannon wasn't giving t'other a lesson in seamanship: in the names of ropes, in the reeving of gear, in the setting of canvas—in twenty things above Mr. Caldwell's tricks of the trade.'

' How was that to be known, sir ? '

' Why, by the sight, by looking, man.
D'ye hear *only* with your ears ? Can't you
get language out of a pointed finger ? '

He broke off and went below, clawing his
way along the rail like a parrot to the head of
the poop ladder.

In all this while they sighted nothing.
The ocean worked in mountains round them.
It was of a lead colour, freckled and frightful,
and every giant sea poured its foaming head
with awful majesty.

On the evening of the fifth day the
weather moderated. At midnight some stars
were shining, the loose scud flew white as
milk, and much about this hour a beautiful
light, that irradiated a wide space of sea and
air, like a little moon, fell out of the heavens
and flashed with a single note of thunder into
the water. This seemed like a signal to the
wind : in twenty minutes it had fallen a stark
calm, and through the dark hours of the

morning the ship lay rolling upon a round vast black swell, without a single pulse of life in her outside the trouble of the sea.

A beautiful dawn: a cloudless day, hot and still. The ocean had wonderfully flattened. The canvas had dried, the planks ran white and hot, the drowned poultry had been hove into the sea. The forecastle was like a laundry yard with sailors' clothes hung up to dry. The ladies came on to the poop after breakfast, looking very pale with their stormy imprisonment of five days. The captain had taken a star in the night, and his own and the observations of the two mates at noon placed the ship far north-west of her course. But detention was the only mischief the gale had wrought. The gallant little ship had sprung from those furious seas into this calm zone without a wrung spar, without a rope-yarn's cost of damage. She was clothed to her trucks in sail again. All gear was hauled taut, everything was in its place, and as she slept, after her conflict, upon the silent roll of the glassy sea, she looked a ship fresh from port.

The moon had grown late, and would not show till after midnight. When the evening closed upon the barque it was a clear liquid dusk, splendid with stars. But their light was not in the air. The captain walked the deck with the Dents, and their conversation was about the arms-chest, the motive of the theft, and the like. The poop at ten o'clock was tolerably well stocked with figures. The mate was in bed. Mr. Poole had the watch, and a lonely shape trudged the forecastle-head.

Two men, pipes in mouth, passed from under the break of the poop and stationed themselves at the foot of the mainmast for a chat and a smoke. It was a warm night, but the place these men had chosen was made pleasant by a refreshing fanning of the main-sail, that hung festooned from its yard. All this particular part of the deck was thick and black with the huge pillar of the mainmast and its lines of gear, belayed to girdling pins, along with other furniture, such as the pump, the winch, and the rest of it hereabouts in the wake of the main hatchway. The two men were Mr. Dike Caldwell and Mr. Patrick Weston. They were both fresh from the cuddy and the grog bottle ; but there was no virtue in whisky to give animation to Caldwell's surly voice.

'I wish,' says Weston, lighting his pipe at a silver tinder-box, then handing the toy to Caldwell, ' that this had been the night fixed on. We're most of us beastly sick of waiting.'

' The weather wasn't to be helped,' said Caldwell.

'I suppose the gold 'll be easy to get at ?' says Weston.

'Hankey knows where it's stowed. Trollope's notion of keeping a couple of men aboard is a good 'un. The whole ten 'll want to go ashore with the gold to make sure of its tomb. The fellows we detain 'll watch the ship whilst we're gone.'

'They may run away with her.'

'That's to be provided against,' said Caldwell, in his slowest, ugliest tone. 'Od's thunder! Don't *you* know sailors?'

'That business of the arms-chest has been a puzzler to some of them,' said Weston. 'Old Benson will come to view it as a miracle. Hankey told me that the blunderbusses made a deuce of a splash as he drove them through the porthole. He says they were real old-fashioned pieces, fit for the Tower of London, bell-mouthed, and wholly worthless, except as weapons to lay about with. Some of the pistols were heavy cavalry affairs, proper to bring a dragoon to his knees on drawing. What's the good of sending a ship to sea armed with such stuff? We might as well have left it alone. There was nothing to be afraid of in that old ore.'

' Best where it is ' said Caldwell gruffly.

' Strange,' continued Weston, raising his voice as though with cheerful spirits, ' that the splashes weren't heard. It was a quiet night too, but every heart was beating at that burning ship.

Caldwell brayed out a sort of laugh. A small wind blew into the sails, and silenced everything aloft. Not a brace needed touching. The ship floated forward with a sudden hush upon the passengers as of enjoyment of the sweet, dew-cold draught.

' I suppose Trollope will stick to to-morrow night ? ' said Weston.

'If it's like this,' answered Caldwell. 'Hand us that tinder-box of yours.'

He chipped in silence, and then sucked at the glow ; meanwhile the people had found their voices again : the breeze made them alive up on the poop. It swelled the cuddy windsail, and Weston, whilst his companion lighted his pipe, watched with an unpleasant

grin upon his distorted face the figure of the
steward, with features silvery with perspiration, put his head into the canvas tube and
stand upright.

'Look at that sight,' said he to Caldwell.
'A boa-constrictor gorging a man!'

'I'm not sure,' said Caldwell, 'that Hallo-
ran Island was the best choice. I'd have
looked further eastward. Saunders, knowing
all about it, settled the thing. But who's to
guess what runs in such a scoundrel's head?'

'Oh, but it can't matter!' exclaimed
Weston peevishly. 'It's too late now. One
island's as good as another if it's unin-
habited, and there's nothing to render it
visitable.'

'Visitable! It's a piece of garden if
Saunders isn't as big a liar as Masters. Just
the sort of place your creeping whaler touches
at for nuts and water. To go and sink three
hundred thousand pounds' worth of stuff in
that shining soil, with the chance of Saunders

failing to keep his appointment in the brigantine. Hush!'

The steward had come out of the windsail and approached them on his way to the forecastle. He stared hard at the two gentlemen, but there was no light to know them by. He passed on, looking backwards once.

'Do you know,' said Weston softly, 'that that curly-legged son of a gun has the scent of us?'

'What then?'

'I wish the blazing business was over,' exclaimed Weston. 'I guess the whole ship distrusts us. We may find ourselves cornered in the wink of an eye. Benson's just the sort of man to take his chance when he's frightened, and that small-arms business *has* frightened the old codger.'

'We are ten,' said Caldwell, in a low, brutal, grunting voice. 'Ten resolved men, whose one opportunity lies in this job. We are in plenty enough to eat up the ship.

How are we to be cornered, as you call
it?'

'Hang it all, man, you *must* know. What's
the use of firearms to a man under hatches?'

'We are too many,' said the other, letting
his head fall back and looking up at the stars.
'Seven could have worked this joke of a ship,
and we keep two of the fo'c'sle hands, and it
isn't ten into three hundred thousand either.
Rot this sort of expeditions! They always
carry a crowd. . . . I say, look at those
shooting stars. Cheap fireworks,' said he,
continuing to stare straight aloft, ' which
there's never a cockney would condescend to
look at. Make a theatre show of it, and the
beasts couldn't swarm fast enough. Perfect
clouds of brilliants, upon my word——'

He felt a hand upon his arm.

'Oh, my great thunder!' exclaimed Weston,
in a whisper of terror, 'every word we've said's
been overheard!'

Caldwell stood stiff and stirless as a graven

image. At this instant the dark, shadowy form of a woman passed from the other side of the mainmast, and went towards the cuddy.

'Who is it?' exclaimed Caldwell, finding his voice and his life too, as it were, in a very flash.

'I didn't see her face,' answered Weston.

Instantly Caldwell was gliding after her. The cuddy entrance was close at hand. The lamps burned brightly. The night was so fine that, though it was now growing late, the ladies and others of the passengers lingered on the poop. The woman looked behind her as she entered the door, and Caldwell perceived that she was Miss Margaret Mansel. He carelessly paced to the foot of the port poop ladder, which he seemed to mount : there standing he commanded a view of the interior. He saw Miss Mansel walk to the table and rest herself upon her hand, with her head turned in the direction of the quarter-deck, and he noticed how quickly she breathed and how white she was.

Weston remained in the shadow of the foot of the mast. It was impossible to mis take the uncertainty and terror expressed by the girl's attitude ; Caldwell continued to watch her. What would she do? Would she go straight with the tremendous secret to the captain? His fingers opened and closed. Fifty horrible fancies worked behind his dark face whilst he held it fastened upon her. She stayed a minute at the table, then stepped round it to her cabin, which she entered.

Caldwell returned quickly to Weston.

'She must be watched,' said he. 'If she would only drop dead? What mumbling, cursed idiots, the others will think us! What's to be done? If she overheard but a quarter, she knows all. Where was she?'

'Just round t'other side. Whilst you were looking at the stars, I heard a movement, and saw her sitting at the foot of the mast. I suppose she was down here for quietude and the fanning of the sail.'

'Was she asleep?'

'By Heaven, no! Did her instantly getting up and walking away look like it?'

'Keep your eye upon her cabin door,' said Caldwell. 'I'll see Trollope. We ought to arm ourselves. She's bewildered, but when she's got her head she'll be off to the captain with the news. Watch—you can see from here, or step closer if you like—whilst I find Trollope and Davenire.'

The man spoke with a subdued voice, but there was the ferocity of the brute-beast in it. His whole figure shook with the fevered strokes of his heart. He walked rapidly to the ladder and gained the poop. The first shape he saw leaning alone, tall and firm against the stars at the rail well forward of the mizzen rigging, was Trollope. One of the mates, he could not tell which, was pacing the weather side of the deck. He heard the

captain's voice aft.   A few ladies were walking near the captain, who stood in conversation with Mr. Dent and his wife.   Half a
dozen figures lounged here and there.   The
dusk was deep, and it was hard to tell a man
till you went close.   But Caldwell instantly
saw Trollope.

'Our secret's out,' said he in a whisper
that seethed through his lips in his efforts to
control its volume.   'Miss Margaret Mansel
knows that we're ten, and mean to seize this
vessel to-morrow night.'

Trollope stood bolt upright.

It's my fault and Weston's.   We were
gabbling like drunken lunatics, but softly in
the darkness down yonder, never doubting
we were alone.   Who in the black fiend's
name should be on the other side of the mast
all the while but Miss Mansel!'

Trollope stood motionless.   He seemed to
have lost his voice.   The sheen from the foremast skylight lay faint on his face, and as

much of his features as was visible looked knotted, black, and distorted, swelling his brow with blood till the tension there forced him to lift his hat, and then he spoke.

'Where is she?'

'In her cabin.'

'You atrocious beasts!'

'I'm madder than you. Mind your words,' said Caldwell in his desperate whisper. 'If ever a devil was in a man's heart, it's here. There's no good in abuse. What's to be done?'

The officer of the watch, who proved to be Mr. Matthews, came across from the other side of the deck and stepped leisurely past, as though to look at them. He then went round the skylight to his former post, and seemed to watch them.

'In her cabin, do you say?' exclaimed Trollope. 'She'll be up in a minute with the news. Perhaps she is waiting for the captain to go below. What made you—*you*, man, of them all so damnably incautious?'

'Look here! there's this to be done, and it's the only thing to do. We must arm our-selves and take the ship to-night.'

Just then Davenire came along from the direction of the wheel. He stopped dead just abreast of them.

'What's wrong?' he exclaimed.

'How do you know that anything's wrong?' said Caldwell, clawing the air as though to subdue the other's strong voice.

'Look at Trollope's attitude. Look at yours. What's wrong, I ask?'

He repeated this question hotly.

'Which is her cabin? Is she out of it?' said Captain Trollope, and he walked to the skylight and put his head into the open frame.

'Miss Mansel has our secret,' said Cald-well. 'I'll tell you how it happened,' and he related the story, tumbling curses into it as he talked.

Davenire grasped him by the arm. He

was a giant of a creature, and the other's arm felt lifeless in that grip of rage.

'I'd like to have the shooting of you both,' said he, letting fall his hand. 'Has the girl gone to the captain yet?'

'If our attitudes are so expressive,' said Caldwell, 'we shan't help ourselves by standing here. There's Matthews over the way watching us, and the captain's still on deck. Come forward.'

Trollope joined them. 'She's not in the cuddy,' said he; 'she doesn't seem to have left her cabin. Have you told Davenire?'

Mr. Cavendish and Mr. Hankey sauntered up.

'This won't do,' said Trollope quickly. 'Davenire, follow me on to the main deck. Caldwell, stop and watch if she leaves her cabin. Don't group yourselves, and be quick with your tale. If the girl makes her report, you and Weston must bounce it out. You'll lie like fiends. She's hysterical, d'ye see?

She's imaginative, she dreams, she works a nightmare into a horrible accusation that must include Dent and Storr.'

Speaking these words swiftly and softly he went on to the quarter-deck, followed by Davenire. He was perfectly collected by this time; Davenire, on the other hand, could scarcely speak for wrath. Weston still watched the cuddy from the foot of the main-mast where the shadow buried him. He quitted his post when Davenire and the other passed.

'I'd have brained her,' said he, 'if I had known she sat there listening.'

'You all-fired dog!' Davenire said.

'What are you doing here?' asked Trollope.

'Watching the cuddy to see if she leaves her cabin,' answered Weston, looking with a mad, helpless eye at Davenire's vast bulk.

'Has she done so?'

'No.'

'Go right aft where the captain is, and let him see you. Talk with a lady if you can find one. You'll have to outswear the girl.'

'The ship should be seized to-night,' said Weston.

'Go aft.'

Weston went slowly up the poop ladder. The other two walked forward. The shadow lay deep near the galley and long boat, and the two continued to pace twenty yards of the deck there. They talked in whispers; the night was so gentle, the air so sweet and warm, that half the watch below, as well as the watch on deck, were nodding in odds and ends of places, and a couple discoursed on the fore-hatch in low growling notes.

'If the girl whips out with it to-night, they'll lock us up one by one whilst we're in our cabins; that's how they'll secure us.'

'The captain durstn't do it on the charge of a girl who might have been dreaming.'

'The idiots mentioned the island, and the value of the nuggets,' said Davenire. 'Could she dream *that?*'

'We're to know nothing of it. We're passengers going home. How can an accusation take effect?'

'I'll tell you what,' growled Davenire. 'If this ship is'nt seized to-night, the game's up.'

'She won't be seized to-night,' answered Trollope coolly, 'and I'll tell you why. Burn and Masters have turned-in drunk as drowned owls. Miss Holroyd's ill, the mother's fidgety, and the surgeon's in and out, and will be in and out through the night. Half the ship's company are sprawling about the decks; how are you going to get them under hatches without more murder than *I* have a mind to for one?'

'They'll be there to-morrow and to-morrow,' said Davenire. 'How *then?* Do you expect everything so to happen as that we may seize this ship sweetly and quietly as though she lay unwatched in dock?'

'I lead in this matter, I think,' said Trollope quickly and fiercely. 'If every man is to be boss, it'll be the fiend's delight with the job all round, and nothing to come of it after.'

'The secret's known, man!' exclaimed Davenire. 'The whole ship'll be full of it.'

'There's nothing to be done to-night,' said Trollope in a steady voice.

Davenire spat in his fury, and made as if he would leave his companion. At this moment Caldwell came off the poop and joined the two.

'She has not left her cabin as yet,' said he, 'and the people are going to bed.'

The three halted, looking aft. The steward was turning out the lamps in the cuddy, leaving one dimly burning. The interior was easily visible from where the men stood. They saw the surgeon come out of one of the berths, and go on deck as though to report to the captain. Mr. Dent stood with Mrs. Storr at the table. But when the colonial merchant had emptied his glass, he shook hands with the lady, and both withdrew.

'If we're not to seize the ship we should turn in,' said Davenire; 'there's Johnson, Shannon, and others on the poop, and the mate's all eyes this night.'

'What's the hour?' said Caldwell.

It was something after eleven.

'I shall loaf about here till midnight,' said Trollope. 'If she keeps her cabin till then, she'll wait for the morning.'

'And then?' said Davenire.

'And then! haven't I said it?' exclaimed the tall man, peering into Davenire's face. 'The fools who have messed us into this must *lie*. What's your hurry besides? We've been blown four hundred miles nor'west. Look at the southing in the course we're now making. Sunday night will be time enough.'

'There'll come no Sunday for this job if to-night's not to begin it,' growled Caldwell in his brutalest accent.

Trollope without answer walked into the cuddy. Whilst he drank some water he stood close beside the girl's door listening for a sound. When he returned to the quarter-deck Davenire and Caldwell had disappeared.

END OF THE FIRST VOLUME

PRINTED BY
SPOTTISWOODE AND CO., NEW-STREET SQUARE
LONDON